THE PRESIDENT'S MAN

The President's Man

by
Elliot Conway

Dales Large Print Books
Long Preston, North Yorkshire,
England.

British Library Cataloguing in Publication Data.

Conway, Elliot
 The President's man.

A catalogue record for this book is
available from the British Library

ISBN 1-85389-645-4 pbk

First published in Great Britain by Robert Hale Ltd., 1995

Copyright © 1995 by Elliot Conway

The right of Elliot Conway to be identified as the author of
this work has been asserted in accordance with the Copyright,
Designs and Patents Act, 1988

Published in Large Print August, 1996 by arrangement with
Robert Hale Ltd.

Dales Large Print is an imprint of
Library Magna Books Ltd.
Printed and bound in Great Britain by
T.J. Press (Padstow) Ltd., Cornwall, PL28 8RW.

In Memory of Charlie Lowther,
a long-time Compadre

PROLOGUE

Ford's Theatre, Washington, Good Friday April 14th, 1865.

The handsome, dark-haired, flamboyantly dressed man strolled into Ford's Theatre, his right hand gripping the butt of a heavy calibre, double-barrelled derringer hidden in his coat pocket. Sweating with fear and excitement at the thought of his self-appointed mission to strike a blow for the now defeated Confederacy, that would shake the victorious Union to the core.

Taking time off from the terrible strains and stresses of leading the Union through four years of bloody civil war, President Lincoln and his wife were having a few relaxed hours at the theatre watching a performance of *Our Country Cousins*. Unchallenged by the Secret Service men, and Union officers guarding the President, the assassin entered the private box and drawing out the pistol put a bullet into the President's brain, mortally wounding him.

Major Henry Rathbone, the President's escort, grappled with the assassin suffering a knife slash across his arm in his gallant attempt to apprehend the killer. The killer then leapt on to the stage and, amid the alarm and confusion the shooting had raised, escaped out of the theatre by a side door and a ready waiting horse. The assassin rode south, across the Potomac to Richmond where he believed he would be welcomed as a hero for killing the arch-enemy of the South.

It was an entrance and exit that would give the actor, John Wilkes Booth, for the first time in his acting life, world-wide notices. Notices he would not enjoy for long. Within hours of the President breathing his last, Booth, trapped in a barn, would put a bullet in his own head.

ONE

The two men, one slicker-garbed, the other with a torn Confederate army-issue waterproof draped over his head, were sitting hunched-shouldered over a spitting angrily, damp-wood fire. The overhanging branches of a twisted-trunk scrub oak under which the two had made their camp offered little protection against the driving rain. Tied up on the other side of the tree were their horses; the steam rising from their still heaving flanks spoke of them having been pushed hard.

From beneath his hat brim, drooping heavy with the rain, Charlie Bannack close-eyed his newly acquired pard. For a man who held his life in his hands Charlie knew very little about him and the all bone, hard-eyed, expressionless face was telling Charlie that this wasn't the time to be asking nosy questions to satisfy his curiosity.

Charlie knew his pard's name, Lars Jackson. Knew that he was a Secret Service agent, one of the President's men. He also knew that Jackson had a lot of worry eating away at his guts. Worry he was now being forced to share. Such as if he stepped out of line Jackson would kill him or see to it that he was killed. In spite of that disturbing thought Charlie could understand the reasoning behind it. The Secret Service had not been able to prevent the crackpot actor, John Wilkes Booth, gunning old Abe Lincoln down in Ford's Theatre but as sure as hell they weren't going to fall down on the job again by letting President Johnson fall to an assassin's bullet. They would kill anyone who even smelt as a possible threat to the President, and that, as Jackson had told him, included him.

Charlie sighed deeply and inched closer to the fire, thinking of how a man gets out of his bed one day to do a certain thing, all mapped out, then fate, luck, whatever, intervenes and he finds himself riding along a trail he never thought existed.

His whole world turned upside down.

That particular day there had been six of them, him, Carl Baker, Billy Law, Josh Cook and the Harland boys. Ex-rebs from the lst Virginia Mounted Infantry, off to rob some Yankee bank. Not that they had ever intended that the raid was to be the start of similar-like activities by a newly raised gang of owlhoots. It was only to have been a one-off job, the Yankee gold they hoped to take being compensation, as they saw it, for the damage and destruction Grant's blue bellies had inflicted on their farms and holdings in the Shenandoah Valley.

The six would-be bank robbers, using back-country trails, forded the Potomac and into Maryland east of Harpers Ferry, with no more advance planning than to rob the bank at Sharpsburg or Hagerstown, depending on which bank seemed the likeliest to hold the most gold in its vault, and the easiest to rob without the shedding of any blood. As desperate as they were to raise themselves a grubstake all of them had seen enough blood spilt the past four years to last them a lifetime.

Lieutenant Harrison had been due for a posting to General Philip H. Sheridan's hard-hitting veterans hammering the rebs into submission west of Richmond, but General Lee's signing the surrender documents at Appomattox Court House prevented him from drawing his sabre in anger. The lieutenant liked to think that his present post, in charge of a detail of cavalry patrolling a section of the Potomac, was as important to the defence of the Union as if he had taken part in the real shooting war with Sheridan's horse soldiers.

It was the opinion of Mr William H. Seward, the Secretary of State, that President Lincoln hadn't been brutally and cowardly slain by one of a small group of fanatical supporters of the South but that the killing was part of the plan of the beaten secessionists to carry on the war by other means, assassinating generals, members of the administration, sending bands of agents north to destroy townships and railroad centres. He had issued orders to the effect that Washington, at least, had to be ringed with blue-belly steel. Lieutenant Harrison had sworn a solemn oath that he would defend Union territory to the death if needs be.

The trooper riding point held up his right hand; Lieutenant Harrison held up his own hand in confirmation of the signal and the column halted. The lieutenant and his sergeant rode up to the crest of the slight rise and drew up alongside the scout.

'Riders down there, moving north, sir,' the scout said. 'All armed up, saw the sun shinin' off shell belts before they rode into those trees. Six of them, I reckon.'

'Good man,' said Lieutenant Harrison as he brought up his glasses and focused them on a spot along the trail where the trees thinned out.

'You're right, Trooper, on both counts,' he said. 'There are six of them, all armed.' He suddenly drew in his breath with a sharp hiss and slowly lowered the glasses and looked at his sergeant. 'Some of them are wearing Johnny Reb tunics.'

'It looks like we've stumbled across some reb sonsuvbitches ridin' out on a raidin' spree, sir,' the sergeant said. 'M'be tryin' to hit some place in Washington by tryin' to sneak into the capital by the back door.'

Lieutenant Harrison put his glasses back into their case, his lips thinning into hard lines of determination. Whatever foul mission those secessionists were embarked on, murder, arson, he would see to it that they would get no further on Union soil to carry it out. Viciously he punched air with his right fist to bring up the column.

'Let's go, Sergeant, and show those sneaky, murdering sons-of-bitches that the war is really over and that they were whupped.'

Billy Law, up front, was the first of them to see the line of horsemen come into view along the low ridge to their right. He twisted ass in his saddle to warn the rest of the boys.

'We ain't broke any laws, yet, Billy,' Charlie said. 'Just smile at them nice and friendly like.' Charlie's smile was stillborn as the blue-belly cavalry came hurtling down the hill at them, yelling and shooting.

'I ain't stoppin' to tell them I ain't broke any laws, Charlie,' Billy yelled. 'They sure don't look as they want to talk! I'm gettin' to hell out of it!'

All thoughts of robbing some bank were forgotten. Crouching low in their saddles, to escape the hail of shells cutting the air about them, the would-be owlhooters rib-kicked their mounts in a desperate life-saving race to put the Potomac between them and their pursuers.

A shell nicked the left front leg of Charlie's mount as it was clearing a small ditch. When it landed the wounded leg gave way causing the animal to lurch sideways in its stride, throwing Charlie over the saddle-horn to hit the ground with a bone-jarring thud. Before he could get on to his feet he was surrounded by the Union cavalry, their pressing-close, high-stepping mounts threatening to pound him into the dirt. Dismounted troopers dragged Charlie upright and though still partly concussed Charlie fought against their rough handling. He heard a voice snarl, 'Take that, you murderous secessionist sonuvabitch!', then felt a heavy blow on the head and a split-second of sickening pain before falling into a deep black pit.

Charlie, head still pounding as though having been kicked by a Missouri mule, scowled painfully at the tall, thin-faced, dude-dressed man eyeing him through the cell bars. 'I'm tellin' you what I told the rest of them!' he said angrily. 'I ain't part of some gang that's aimin' to kill President Johnson, General Grant or any other blue-belly chief. I didn't even know that Abe Lincoln had been killed; I've been travelling along the back trail this past week. But I'm right sorry to hear about it. It must have been some crazy bastard to shoot a man down in front of his own wife. No ex-reb soldier, how much he hated what Abe Lincoln stood for, would cold-bloodedly shoot him down.'

'You and the men who were riding with

you were armed and on Union soil,' Lars Jackson said. 'What were we supposed to think? Right now everyone in Washington is chasing shadows. The Secretary of State thinks that every Southerner from Jeff Davis and General Robert E. Lee right down to fellas like you are plotting to murder every member of President Johnson's administration. He won't wear it that the men involved in the killing, we've managed to rope most of them in, were only a small bunch of secessionist fanatics. What makes it more galling to us was that between them they hadn't the brains to pull off a successful holdup of a general store but the sonsuvbitches had the luck or whatever to assassinate the President right under our very noses. And there could be more crackpots somewhere out there hoping they too have the same kind of luck. As I said we're being run ragged.' Lars thin-smiled Charlie. 'You're durn fortunate you were not shot out of hand. It was only because the officer who caught you had the sense to bring you in alive for interrogation or you would have been in a hole in the ground by now.'

Charlie couldn't disagree with what the thin-faced man had told him. When he had come to, strapped head down over a trooper's horse, he'd seen the fish-eyed looks the blue bellies were giving him and knew that he was hovering over the thin line between living and ending up dead. And in the jailhouse, the guards all but throwing him down the stairs that led to the cell block, chaining his hands and legs as though he was a caught runaway slave, he was still getting the same shit-scary glances.

Then came the constant questioning by two, sometimes three men. Each question punctuated by a boot in the ribs or a fist in the pit of his stomach that caused Charlie so much pain that he wished they had finished him off for good when they jumped him.

'Yeah, I reckon the blue bellies were right to be suspicious-like of me and the boys,' Charlie said grudgingly. 'But that don't alter the fact that none of us were mixed up in the killin' of Mr Lincoln or had it in our minds to do the same to some other Unionist politicians. The war ended for us the day old Robert E. Lee signed that piece of paper. And that's the gospel truth, mister. Even if the guards out there start kickin' the shit outa me again it wouldn't change what I've told you any.'

'What the hell then did you intend doing coming across the Potomac loaded for bear?' asked Lars.

Charlie hesitated a moment before answering. 'Ah, hell,' he said. 'You might as well know, it ain't goin' to put me in a deeper hole than I'm in right now. Me and the boys were reckonin' on holding up a Yankee bank. Just one. We opined that you Yankees owe us for all the damage Grant's wild boys did to our places in the Shenandoah Valley.'

'Well, I'll be damned,' Lars murmured, then gave Charlie a long assaying look. He was, by profession, a good judge of character. An ability that had saved his neck operating behind the reb lines during the war. In Mr Bannack's eyes, a man he reckoned only half his age, and a great deal shorter in height, he saw frightened anger. Natural, in the circumstances the kid knew he was in. He could see no signs of the shiftiness and evasiveness of a forked-tongue. Mr Bannack was speaking the truth and Lars came to a decision. 'Open up the cell door, guard,' he said. 'And take those irons off then leave us on our own.'

Lars sat down on the cot alongside Charlie and handed him a packet of Bull Durham and a paper. 'Smoke?' he said.

Charlie gave him a lopsided, painful apology of a grin. 'You'd better roll me one, mister. My hands are kinda shaky, those irons ain't no featherweight. And the welcome I got off the guards here ain't what a fella would call a "welcome home" reception.'

Lars waited till Charlie had pulled on the cigarette several times before he spoke again.

'Mr Bannack,' he said. 'I believe what you've just told me, that you had nothing to do with John Wilkes Booth and his bunch of crazies. So I am going to offer you a deal that will get you out of the cell and free of any charges. Will you hear me out?'

Charlie took in another lungful of tobacco smoke. Wary-eyed he said, 'I'm listening.'

'My name is Lars Jackson,' Lars began. 'Chief agent of the Secret Service, responsible for security in Washington. The President's men....'

Charlie had the urge to tell Mr Lars Jackson that the Secret Service had made a balls-up of protecting old Abe Lincoln but he kept his peace wanting to hear about a deal that would get him out of this prison while he could still walk about on his own two feet unaided.

'Our big job at the moment, as you'll rightly guess, Mr Bannack,' continued Lars, 'is to make certain that we've roped in all the conspirators who were involved in the plot to kill Mr Lincoln. We thought we had till one of my men found a letter hidden in Booth's clothes when they were getting him ready for burial. It was from someone who called himself M and was posted in Kansas City, Kansas. All it said was, "Success in your great enterprise". We reckon that the "great enterprise" the letter speaks of was the conspirators original plan to kidnap Mr Lincoln and take him down to Richmond. Speculating a little further, we opine that this fella M could be the man who put up the cash for the kidnap scheme. Paid for the horses, the guns, and whatever else Booth and his followers needed.'

Charlie was still all ears. He couldn't figure out yet what Mr Jackson's deal was, but he would try and jump over the Potomac if that's what the deal was if it meant him getting free. 'I take it that you intend going down to Kansas City to try and find the bankrolling Mr M, Mr Jackson,' he said.

Lars nodded. 'I know it's a long-odds shot finding him but we've got to try. The snag is that in the Kansas/Missouri border country ex-rebs and ex-Union men are practically rubbing shoulders with each other now the fighting's finished. I could end up talking to men who shed blood for the South, and get shot for my pains. Or asking a Copperhead, a man who swears he was for the Union but secretly he favoured and helped the Confederates, for information and I would meet the same early death. It will be a long time in that part of the country before the hate men feel for each other dies away. This is where you can help out, Mr Bannack. You can ask questions of people I couldn't approach.'

'Me! A Yankee spy!' Charlie gasped.

'Not a spy, Mr Bannack, a temporary President's man,' Lars said. 'General Lee said that the war was over for the South and we've got to begin to live as one nation again. That was Mr Lincoln's hopes. But this fella, M, doesn't want that, he's still got the big hate and he'll grubstake any bunch of crackpots that intend to finish what Booth and his friends began. So you won't be breaking any faith with the South. It's a damn sight better than rotting in jail and you'll be paid an agent's salary. If we get real lucky and you get me near enough to M for me to arrest him then you can go and rob that bank or whatever and I won't lift a finger to stop you.'

Charlie ground the cigarette butt under the heel of his boot. Lars Jackson's proposition didn't need much weighing up. In fact no thought at all. It was jail or freedom, of a sorts. The Secret Service man had him well and truly over a barrel. 'I'll ride with you to Kansas City, Mr Jackson,' he said. 'Though I can't see you getting close to Mr M with or without my help. But I reckon for you, like it was for me in the army, orders are orders and, as you stated, sometimes long odds come up.'

Lars smiled again. 'Good,' he said. Then, as suddenly as it had come, the smile was gone and Charlie saw the fierce-eyed look the blue-belly troopers and the prison guards had given him on the hard, thin face. 'If you are contemplating ditching me along the trail some place or sell me out to a still sore-loser reb, I'd advise you to think again, Mr Bannack. If anything happens to me that can be put down as your doing your likeness will be posted on wanted flyers from here to the Rio Grande with a price tag on them of five thousand dollars. You'll never be able to sleep with both eyes closed or ride without a crick in your neck with looking along your back trail for the dust of a bounty hunter closing in on you.' The smile swiched back on again, more warmth and humour in it this time. 'Nothing personal, Mr Bannack. It's just that I think that it is foolish for a man to take more risks than he has to. Getting myself needlessly killed won't help the President any.'

'No offence taken, Mr Jackson,' Charlie replied. 'It's only natural for a man to look out for himself.'

Lars got up from the cot and called for the guard to open the cell door. 'I'll go and get your release papers signed, Mr Bannack. Shouldn't take more than an hour. Then you can clean up and get sworn in as an agent.' Lars called to the guard to bring Mr Bannack something to eat. 'And a bottle of whiskey and don't bother to lock the cell door or put the irons back on him, he's a Federal agent, or soon will be.'

The last thirty miles to the Missouri/Kansas

border had to be made on horseback. Some of the trestle bridges on the railroad were still out. Blown up or burnt down by rebs or blue bellies, Charlie couldn't say. There had been a lot of dirty infighting in south-west Missouri during the war. Although the State had never officially left the Union its many Confederate supporters were busy shedding Union blood way back in '58. The rain hit them before they had travelled six miles from the rail depot and Lars Jackson decided to make camp. Charlie smiled to himself. The Washington desk-bound dude would be wet and sore-assed before they crossed the Kansas river. A smile showed on his face when he recollected that he had ridden out to rob a Union bank and had ended up as a blue-belly Government agent sworn to protect the blue-belly President's life, with his own if that was called for. Charlie's smile sickened and faded away.

Without lifting his gaze from the fire Lars said, soft and conversationally, 'Men approaching the camp, Mr Bannack. More than three of them.' His voice, still low, sharpened. 'Don't move, stay as you are!'

Wild-fear chills ran up Charlie's back as he fought the urge to swing round and face a possible threat. It could be that the men were innocent travellers like themselves but Charlie wasn't buying that. It was dangerous territory they were riding through. Ex-soldiers, from both sides of the war, who had lost all, homes, land, families, were taking up thieving, killing if desperate enough, to get by. He had started along that trail himself. On the old soldier's maxim that it didn't hurt to prepare for the worst Charlie drew out his pistol and gently and quietly thumbed back the hammer, holding it ready for instant action under his waterproof. He nodded slightly to Lars to signify he was ready for whatever play they would have to make and got back an answering bob of Lars' head. Charlie looked at Lars with a heap more respect now. For a desk man he had good ears. He was just picking up the sounds of their approaching night visitors. They were closing in Indian-style, sneaky and quiet, which proved to Charlie that they were up to no good. It hadn't been a wasted effort drawing his gun.

He heard the ominous double snick of a rifle lever being worked and looked across at Lars Jackson. The Secret Service man was still unmoving as an Indian. A voice as menacing as the sound of the rifle being worked said, 'Just sit tight, pilgrims, and neither of you will get hurt.'

Charlie sensed that there was another man with the rifle man, no doubt drawing a bead on him as well. He hadn't a cat in hell's chance of swinging round and taking two men on. Suddenly he saw movement behind Lars Jackson and picked out the shape of another man, the flickering firelight reflecting off a held-across-the-chest rifle. His life as a Secret Service agent seemed to be ending the same way his life as a potential bank robber had, only more permanently. The only option this time was whether he ended up in heaven or hell. Charlie gritted his teeth. If the stone-faced Mr Jackson wasn't prepared to make a fight of it he was. He'd be damned if he would go down without taking company with him.

Two red streaks of flame burst through Lars' coat, the two sharp Colt cracks made Charlie flinch with shock. Then it was his move as the man behind Lars swung his rifle round and down. Charlie's single shot punched a hole in his forehead, sending the man stumbling back. Lars' shot fired an instant later flung the already dead man into the blackness of the brush, out of Charlie's sight.

Charlie, pistol out in the open, turned and saw two dark bundles on the ground only feet away from him. One unmoving, the other groaning and writhing. Charlie got to his feet and stepped over to him just in time to hear the man's last throaty gasp for life-giving air before he too lay still. A strain-faced Charlie looked over the fire at Lars standing over the man he had shot. 'Any more around, Mr Jackson?' he asked.

Lars shook his head. 'I don't think so, Mr Bannack.'

Charlie eased the hammer of his pistol

forward then sheathed it. He gave Lars a tight-faced grimace. 'I owe you an apology, Mr Jackson. I'd thought you'd frozen up on me being that you don't come up against many sneaky, bushwhackin' sonsuvbitches in Washington. I was wrong, dead wrong. You're as good with a gun as any man I've seen.'

'I had to wait till both of them were side by side,' Lars said. 'Both of them had to go down together.' He smiled. 'I was a mite worried that you wouldn't get the man behind me so both of us were wrong.' Lars close-eyed Charlie. 'Has it upset you killing them, Mr Bannack?'

'Kinda,' replied Charlie. 'I ain't killed rebs before.'

'They could have been "bummers", the no-good scavengers who followed Sherman's army, drifting north for easier pickings. Sherman's issued orders that all looters are to be shot on sight. Whoever they were, they had in their hearts to kill us, Mr Bannack.'

'Yeah, I suppose you're right, Mr Jackson,' Charlie said. 'You've got to play the cards as they fall and we sure didn't start this game. What do we do with them?'

'Strap them across their horses,' Lars replied. 'The horses will find people. M'be Christian-minded folk who will see that they are decently buried. If we report the shootings to the law all the paperwork will delay us. More serious to our well-being, those three dead men might have kin or close friends hereabouts and we could have a blood feud on our hands.'

'You sure don't let anything stand in your way, Mr Jackson,' Charlie said.

Lars' face became all bony angles. 'There's a president's life at stake, Mr Bannack; I can't afford not to. It could get rougher.' He thin-smiled Charlie. 'Thinking that you've made a bad deal, Mr Bannack?'

'I've made worse ones,' Charlie replied. 'Leastways General Picket made one for me when he told us Virginians that we could push the blue-belly line off Cemetery Ridge with no sweat at all. Of course, the old bastard didn't mention all the blood we would spill tryin' to do it, and still failed.' Charlie grinned at Lars. 'I like being around fancy shootin' gents. Kinda makes me feel protected.'

Lars didn't tell Charlie that if he had thrown in with the horse thieves by blurting out that he was a bankrobber being taken to Kansas City by a Federal agent he would have shot him dead first and taken his chance with the other three. He knew now that he had no longer to worry about Mr Bannack's loyalty to the oath he had sworn back in Washington. He was as committed as he was in tracking down Booth's paymaster. Instead he said, 'Let's do what we have to do and break camp, Mr Bannack. Someone may have heard the shooting.'

TWO

Thomas Magnus Lindford was a big-bellied, florid-faced, hail-friend, well-met man. His all out support for the Union cause in the State's 'dark and bloody days', and when the real, big war had started was an inspiration to the Kansas border folk. The talk of the saloon-drinking clientele. Even the State Governor when entertaining Union Army top brass at dinner parties would relate of how, 'That old all-balls sonuvabitch, Thomas M. Lindford, had a Union flag flying on his chimney stack defying, nay damn it, daring by George, Quantrill and Bloody Bill Anderson and their "black flag" no-quarter boys to ride out of their hole-ups across in Missouri to come and tear it down. A man solid for the Union, gentlemen. A man Abe Lincoln would be proud to shake his hand.'

Thomas M. Lindford was also a Copperhead. Yet his secret support for the Confederates wasn't because he favoured their cause. He didn't give a damn about the for and against the right of a State to be pro or anti-slave, the right to leave the Union. Issues that had set kin against kin. The only cause he believed in was that of making Thomas M. Lindford richer, a power in the State of Kansas. Like all men successfully clawing their way to the top of the pile he could see future trends. Land, once the war had started, was going for a song. Nowhere more so than here along the Kansas/Missouri border where sodbusters were being driven off their properties by pro-South Missouri raiders. They were willing to sell their land cheap to any quick buyer so that they and their families could get to hell out of what was becoming a killing ground.

Once the war ended good growing land would soon regain its true value but Lindford didn't want to be sitting on a pile of leases that could be in jeopardy if the South, a government not friendly inclined towards the State of Kansas, won. Unable to foresee the outcome of the war and being that he only gambled on certainties, Lindford backed both horses in the war game. Defiantly showing the Union flag and giving generously to the Union war charities at the same time he was supplying arms and food and military information to the Missouri irregulars.

Lindford wanted nothing from the Union other than being accepted as a Union patriot. From the South he wanted something more substantial. Such as when the reb guerillas were not out raiding genuine Union military targets they were to raid farmers and homesteaders whose holdings he wanted to build up his land empire. To keep up the pretence of being a committed Unionist the guerillas would occasionally raid his place, burn down a barn, empty of course, destroy a few acres of growing corn and shatter a few windows in the big house with gunfire.

So that when he paid a visit to a farmer to commiserate with him over the loss of his livestock and the house that the farmer had all but sweated his balls off to build now only a smoking ruin, he could, mealy-mouthed say, 'I know how you feel, neighbour', and shed crocodile tears of sympathy. Then he would drop the hint that strong Unionist supporter that he was, if he'd a family he would as hell like to stay in this Godforsaken territory and risk having them being harmed by those sons-of-bitches, Quantrill's marauders. Adding, 'If you feel like pulling up stakes, neighbour, I'll buy your land from you. You'll rightly appreciate, owing to the war and the raiding and all, it isn't worth a great deal but I'll pay you enough so that you can get your family a long ways west, away from the fighting.'

When the war finally ended Lindford owned a great deal of land. A few of the farmers had refused to sell out to him even though they had lost all they possessed, including close kin, as a result of the raids. Those stubborn sons-of-bitches lived in soddies, holes in the ground so that they could stay and work their land. Not that their few acres would boost his vast holdings all that much but not getting them blighted his grand dreams. His greed and pride made him want all the apple, skin, core and pips as well.

Booth's mad-assed scheme of kidnapping President Lincoln fitted in with Lindford's way of thinking. Not that he thought it would succeed and even if Booth managed by some miracle or other pull it off it wouldn't start the war all over again. The South had had a bellyful of death and destruction. It would, however, he reasoned, stir up the fears of the few farmers left in the border regions that things could take a turn for the worst. That they still couldn't sleep easy in their beds at night or concentrate all their daytime hours into productive labour on their land. Bringers of the killings and burnings they had lived with for so long could at any moment again come ass-kicking, whooping and a'hollering through the brush along the river bottom lands.

Lindford knew that many of the guerilla bands didn't accept that the war was over, indeed some of them were still fighting pitched battles with the Union troops who were hunting them down. Others, who were reluctantly eating crow could be easily persuaded, if the dollars were forthcoming, to carry on with their raiding. Raids which could force the diehard sodbusters to have second thoughts about staying on their land.

Lincoln's assassination gave the whole South the fear-shits. That his killing would sick Grant's and Sherman's blue-belly armies on them. The news had also made his bowels loosen; after all he had helped to finance the son-of-a-bitch's operation, sent him a letter wishing him every success. No one was more pleased to learn of Booth's death, before he could be made to talk, than he was. Not that he had any fear of Booth fingering him if he had lived. Though, on reflection, it had been unwise of him to have written to Booth. It was just that he had a lot riding on Booth's original scheme of kidnapping Lincoln and hadn't wanted him to chicken-out of his stated mission when the crunch came.

His link with Booth had been with

another Copperhead who had told him of Booth's plan and the need of cash to buy guns, rent for safe houses etc. That man had died of a heart attack on hearing of Lincoln's assassination. No doubt, Lindford opined, brought on by the fearful realization that the natural revulsion felt by ordinary people, ex-rebs and Unionists alike, against anyone who had anything to do with the killing, would be that the hunt for Booth's accomplices would be nationwide and determined. One day the hunters could come knocking at his front porch door. The way Lindford saw it, fortuitously all his connections with the assassins had been severed.

It was an ill wind that doesn't blow someone some good, Lindford thought. All he had to do was to make contact with the Missouri hold-outs and get them to raise hell this side of the line and he would be able to snap up the leases that had eluded him for so long. Sweet-talking to their owners was over.

'I'll help you to build the house again,

41

Pa,' Liz Downes said. 'Why Ma and the boys would turn over in their graves if you decided to quit the valley. The war is over, they'll be no more raidin'.'

Caleb Downes, sitting alongside his daughter on the wagon, looked at the stone chimney stack, all that was standing that could be recognized as once being part of a house, the house where he and his wife had raised their family. His gaze drifted beyond the ruins of the house, higher, on to the windswept ridge and the lonesome graves of Ma, and their two boys, Clem and Joe. The three of them killed the night the Missouri brush boys came with dynamite and cans of coal oil. The sons-of-bitches killed everything that drew breath on his holding except him and Liz.

He had been lucky not to have been killed alongside them though many a day since that night, living, while they were lying cold up there on the ridge, had become a curse, almost too much to bear. Blaming himself for their deaths. If he had only accepted Mr Lindford's offer for his land, low as it was, all his family would have still been alive. A marauder's shell had creased his skull, laying him out cold. He knew no more till Liz was leading him out of the root cellar, still dazed, and picking his way through the smoking timbers and dynamite blasted 'dobe walls. And Liz telling him that Ma and the boys were somewhere beneath it all. He wanted to end his life there and then. Liz, face soot-smeared, dress all torn and singed, glared angrily at him with smoke-reddened eyes. 'Ma didn't tell me to take you down into the cellar just so that you could kill yourself when you came out again!' she yelled at him. 'She knew that unless she could do something none of us were going to get out alive. You getting laid low gave her the chance to save two lives. I wanted to stay and use a gun but she said that the Missouri scum weren't going to take all her children from her. And you, Pa, would need someone to look after you, so that you could get blood for blood for what the Missourians were doing to us.'

Caleb looked back at his daughter and hardly knew her as being part of him. She had changed that much. Thinned out a lot, face all eyes, wildness at the back of them ready to flare alive at any upset. Strong-minded as any man, white or red, and still brimful of hate for the Missourian raiders.

'It'll mean haulin' at least two wagon loads of timber, Liz,' he said. 'Though I reckon there's plenty of stone around for the walls. If you intend stayin' out here to give me a hand it will mean you spending cold nights sleeping in the wagon.'

Liz's face softened, womanly, in a smile. She put her arms round her father and kissed him. 'I come from plains-folk stock, Pa. I'll stay with you and Ma and the boys. We'll get the house built all that sooner before the winter sets in.

Charlie and Lars split up on the outskirts of Kansas City to book themselves into separate rooming houses.

'I'll be tending bar in the Plains saloon, Mr Bannack,' Lars said. 'You can contact me there if you think you've got a lead on Mr M.' He grinned at Charlie. 'Or even a smell of one. I won't be upset if it turns out to be a false trail, we'll get a heap of those. But all the information we pick up will have to be thoroughly checked out. That's what we're here for.'

'How the heck do I get a lead on this fella?' Charlie asked angrily. 'I ain't no spy. Do I ask every man I meet if he sent a letter to John Wilkes Booth?'

'There's nothing to being a spy, Mr Bannack,' Lars said soothingly. 'All it requires is to be able to move among folk without drawing attention to yourself with both ears flapping. If you're lucky someone, in someplace or other, in conversation with another fella, a bawdy-house whore m'be, could mention that they knew the man who shot the President real well. Then we can check him out, right back to the day he came kicking and squalling into the world, to find out whether it's only blowhard talk or he really did know Booth. Then we ask him if he knows the names of any good friends of Booth. We round them up then start checking them out. If we get lucky we could meet up with this fella M. It's a slow, ball-aching job. My advice would be to drift along the border valleys. There's ex-rebs there, on both sides of the line. Some of them may be right happy that Booth killed old Abe and pleased enough to talk about it to another ex-reb. You could get a lead on the man we're after. You can never tell in this game, Mr Bannack, where your next lead is going to come from, or who will give it to you.'

Still only part convinced that he had what it took to be a Secret Service agent, Charlie, after being wished, 'Good luck', left Lars to find himself a room for the night, then to get some rations in for his trip along the border country.

THREE

Augustus Freedman waited till the man he was waiting for had entered the saloon and sat down at a table in a darkly lit alcove before he picked up the bottle of whiskey and the two glasses from the bar and walked over and joined him. Freedman was a plump, city-suited man, a smaller version of his present boss, Thomas M. Lindford. His previous boss had been the head of a special department of the short-lived Confederate States of America. Like Lars Jackson he had been a Secret Service agent, a spy, working out of Missouri, passing on intelligence the local guerilla bands had picked up concerning the disposition of Union forces to Confederate HQ.

Now that the war had ended, and not too happy about the outcome, still carrying the hate for the Union cause, he worked for one of his wartime contacts, Lindford. He was still carrying on the war, and getting a damn sight better paid for doing so.

Mason, the reason for Freedman being in Macey's bar, Lawrence, Kansas, was a medium-built, pinched-face, weasel-eyed man, a leader of a bunch of former Border Ruffians. Although entered in Confederate Army lists as irregulars fighting under the folds of the 'Bonny Blue' flag, Mason's boys took time off from planned military actions to line their own pockets, killing, burning, looting anyone they thought was worth the sweat of the effort. Unionist or Confederate. So much so that before the war ended the Southern military authorities were seeking to hang Mason and his guerillas for the crimes of arson and murder.

Freedman poured out two drinks. Mason picked up his glass and downed it in one. Freedman poured him another whiskey. It vanished in a similar effortless gulp. The liquor seemed to loosen up Mason somewhat. He smiled, an all-tooth, mirthless exercise, in keeping with his weasel eyes. Looking around the bar he said, 'I burnt this place down, twice. Once in '58, then again with Captain Quantrill during the war.' Mason's grin widened, almost reaching his stone-cold eyes. 'We killed nigh on two hundred Nigra-lovin' sonsuvbitches that day.'

Freedman filled Mason's glass for the third time, impatient to get the business in hand over as quickly as possible. It was dangerous for him to be talking to Mason for any length of time in front of people, who, if Mason got caught by the law and his likeness and killing record made public, could recollect to the authorities the description of the man Mason had drinks with in Macey's bar. The South was in no position to hunt down Mason and see him strung up high but the Union Army had every intention of sending the former Missouri brush boy to hell to meet up with Quantrill and 'Bloody' Bill Anderson and the rest of the guerillas who had paid the price for their bloodthirsty ways. Mason's more immediate danger to his well-being, thought Freedman sourly, was that, inflamed by the whiskey he was pouring down his throat, the crazy son-of-a-bitch could take it in his head to put Lawrence to the torch for the third time.

Freedman, satisfied that he wouldn't upset Mason by cutting in on his drinking too soon, cast a glance about him to see if the other drinkers in the bar were fully occupied with their own pleasures before he placed a bag of gold coins on the table near Mason's drinking hand. 'The place you've got to hit is the Downes farm, south of Red Deer creek. Should be no problem to you and your boys, there's only an old man and his daughter there. They've just moved back on to their land.'

Mason favoured Freedman with another one of his toothy blood-chilling smiles, wondering briefly just who the hell was the man with the gold the little dude was doing the running about for. 'Ain't it a cryin' shame all that sweat they'll be raisin' workin' the land will be wasted. M'be the daughter can be persuaded to raise a sweat for me. I can allus hang her pa if she won't oblige.'

Freedman made his excuses, leaving Mason to finish off the rest of the whiskey. It had always been a dirty business he was in. Now it was getting dirtier. What honour there had been in it, when he could tell himself that all the killings and burnings had been for the Confederacy's right to exist as an independent nation, no longer applied. Realistically, opined Freedman, that short-lived fact was now history. There could be no turning back of the clock no matter how many presidents were assassinated. He shrugged his shoulders as if to dismiss his thoughts. What the hell if he had lost his honour, he could still hurt the blue-belly sons-of-bitches. And he still had his loyalty. He had eaten Lindford's salt, taken his gold. If he ordered him to make a deal with the Devil himself he would do it. Freedman cold-smiled. He had just done so, with Mason. Satan in all but horns and forked-tail.

FOUR

Liz Downes came round from the tailgate of the wagon carrying two mugs of coffee and found her way blocked by a pair of roughly dressed men. Men, she opined, who had not ridden up to the part-built house by way of the main trail then dismounted and walked across to the wagon, but had come on to her through the brush which had grown wild over the years the land had lain unattended. That their intentions were anything but good neighbourly was shown in the bloodcurdling cruel-faced smiles both men were giving her.

Liz gasped out aloud in alarm, dropped the mugs of coffee, and reached frantically over the side of the wagon for her pa's rifle. The smaller of the two men struck her a blow across the face with the back of his hand that bounced her, crying with pain, against the wagon. Dizzy-headed, tasting the saltiness of blood in her mouth, she would have fallen if the man who had dealt her the blow hadn't grabbed her by the waist and spun her round to face him. Her sickness reached right down to the pit of her stomach. She had never gazed into such frightening, evil eyes.

The marauder clutched at her ass with a hand that burnt her flesh through the thickness of her pants and drawers like a red-hot iron. He pulled her close to him, flattening her breasts against his bony chest. And Liz saw her dreadful fate confirmed in the widening of her molester's merciless eyes. A pistol shot made Liz twist her head round and she saw her pa lying on the ground with three more of the raiders standing over him. A raging blaze of anger swept over her and she ignored her own plight. 'You scum!' she cried. 'You've shot my pa!' And spat into her captor's face, struggling fiercely to break free from his grip.

Mason cursed and brought up a hand in a tight, hard fist and caught Liz a blow on the jaw that knocked her unconscious. He let go of her and she slid to the ground to lie at his feet in a crumpled heap. He dried his face with the back of his coat sleeve and, looking down at Liz, said, 'You'll sure have to work real good and pleasant for me not to harm you. Keep an eye on her, Slim, while I go over and see if her pa has been persuaded that takin' up farming again in this part of Kansas ain't good for his health.'

'Why don't we just plug the sodbuster for keeps, boss?' Slim said.

'Why?' replied Mason. 'The "why" is because this ain't just a raid. This is a bona fide business transaction between the sodbuster, though he don't know it, and a certain party who wants the paper the sodbuster holds entitling him to this piece of dirt. We're here to speed up that sale for our client. If we kill the sodbuster the shysters will only pass the land deeds on to some other of the sodbuster's kin then we'll have to haul-ass across here again to frighten whoever the sonuvabitch is into making the sale.' Mason smiled at Slim. 'Business deals don't allus run smooth-like.'

Charlie saw a blue haze of wood-fire smoke rising lazily above the tree tops that lined the left-hand side of the trail. Too thick to be a regular campfire smoke. More likely some farmer clearing his land, burning a heap of brush and tree roots. He had taken Lars' advice and was riding along the border trail. His achievement in his new role as a Union secret Service agent had been one fat zero. He hadn't met any farmer or traveller along the trail to even pass the time of day with, let alone, without raising any suspicions, find out who still held strong feelings about wanting to see the whole of the Union government in Washington shot down and m'be get a lead of some sorts on the whereabouts of Mr M., and just who the son-of-a-bitch was. Charlie reckoned that he was wasting his time, but that was Mr Jackson's concern, he had told him he was no spy, but would still press on regardless, living up to his end of the bargain.

The number of broken-down shacks

and barns, the run-to-wild land that had once been cultivated, puzzled Charlie. He thought by now their owners would have returned from the war and been working on the land and rebuilding their derelict homes. They couldn't all have been killed. Unless of course some of the Missouri brush boys were still in business, carrying on with their raiding and burning. Charlie's spirits rose at the sight of the smoke. It seemed at least one man had survived the war and had taken up being a farmer again.

He pulled his horse off the trail and nosed it along a narrow track that twisted its way through the brush and trees in the general direction of the fire. On hearing the pistol discharge, habits formed over the war years came automatically into play. In a flash Charlie was out of his saddle, rifle in hand, and moving fast but silently in a crouching run to the edge of the brush, in time to see a young girl being punched to the ground and the man who had done the hitting walking across to three other members of the gang, one of them kicking at a man lying stretched out on the ground.

Charlie tagged the five men as Missouri raiders. Men who had no doubt whooped it up on hearing of Abe Lincoln getting shot. Men who Lars Jackson had told him to get close to and keep his ears open to all their talk on the long-shot chance of getting a lead on Mr M. Charlie had other ideas. He knew that Lars Jackson, as a Secret Service agent, would sacrifice his life and his own, his grandmother's if she was still alive, to protect the President's life. That was his duty as he saw it. Charlie didn't see events in such a broad, national frame. All he saw was a girl being beaten brutally to the ground and the fearful ordeal she would go through when she came to having five men use her for their pleasure. She was in greater danger than the President sitting in the White House surrounded by armed Secret Service men. He would be lower than a mangy cur dog if he rode away and left her to her fate.

Charlie levered a shell into the chamber of his seven-load Spencer, a spoil of war taken from a dead blue-belly horse soldier, and drew a bead on the hatchet-faced girl-beater now standing talking with the three hardcases beside the fire. The man wasn't the best of targets, the smoke from the big brush fire kept gusting over the four men and to get in real close to pull off a killing-shot would mean him having to come out into the open. Then it could be him catching a killing-shot.

Charlie wasn't a natural-born killing-man but he was about to go up against men who couldn't be scared off by the sound of rifle shells whistling around their ears. He would have to down at least two of them for keeps otherwise they would scatter and knowing that only one gun was firing on them close in on him. Charlie didn't want a real battle on his hands against odds he couldn't hope to beat.

Mason moved at the same instant as Charlie squeezed the trigger of the Spencer. The shell tore a jagged hole through the brim of his hat and hit the marauder behind him full in the face, knocking him backwards on to the fire, a dead man

58

before the flames caught at his clothes. Charlie cursed as a billow of smoke and sparks the fallen body had raised blotted out not only his original target but also the other two men. Twisting round on his belly Charlie brought his rifle on to the marauder beside the girl, catching him between the shoulders with a single shot before he could reach the shelter of the wagon, stretching him out on the ground choking to death on his own blood.

The other marauders had quickly got over the initial shock of coming under unexpected and deadly fire and shells were ripping the leaves off the brush close to Charlie. Charlie opined that he had catalogued the men right. Hard-asses who couldn't be easily frightened off. Although he had lost the edge of surprise Charlie reckoned that he still held a slight advantage. He had forced the men to seek cover behind a knee-high wall, pinning them down in a tight little group. Not for long he thought soberly. Soon one of them would make a break for it under the covering fire of the other two and try and outflank him. Charlie did some fast thinking.

A whole regiment, a company detail, three no-good assholes like those skulking behind that wall, under pressure, Charlie knew, were only as strong as their leader. Down him and the rest would lose the stomach to continue the fight. He had seen it happen. He had also seen men hanging on till there was no one left alive to fight. Whatever. Charlie thought that it was the only choice he had before they took it in their heads to come and flush him out.

Charlie plumped for the leader of the marauders as the man he had missed with his first shot. If he wasn't he deserved shooting for hitting a girl. If he couldn't pick him off any one of the other two would have to do. Realizing that they were down three men, and could suffer more losses, might make them break.

Charlie wriggled back, deeper into the brush, before getting to his feet and running to a position from where he could get an angle shot at the marauders. He heard shells peppering the spot he had just vacated. His luck was still with him. He dropped down and took a quick look through the brush. And discovered that his luck had just run out. He still couldn't get a clear shot at any of the marauders unless he moved further left to clear the wall and that was open ground and sudden death. Charlie had another quick think before the marauders realized that they were firing at shadows and made their own plans.

He pumped three rapid shots at the wall behind the marauders sheltering wall. Not in frustrated anger at not being able to draw a bead on any of them but in cold, calculating speculation. Opining that the splinters kicked off the stone or ricocheting shells might do the wounding or killing a direct shot would do. Before the ringing sound of the last shot had faded away Charlie glimpsed the upper torso of one of the marauders. Whether his plan had worked or the man was shifting round to take him on didn't matter. He had a target, bossman or not. Time was running out too fast for him to be disappointed if it wasn't.

Charlie aimed and fired and saw the whole man rear up into view, clutching at his right shoulder face twisted in pain. Charlie gave a grim smile. Lady Luck had returned. The man he had wounded was the thin-faced bastard. Now he was getting a taste of what he had dished out to the girl; ball-shrivelling pain. The two remaining marauders leapt up and blazed away at him with fast-firing pistols and Charlie ate dirt.

The firing died away and Charlie raised his head and risked a look at the shack, in time to see the three marauders hastily mounting their horses, the one he had wounded being helped into his saddle by one of his compadres. Charlie worked the Spencer's locking lever to bring the last load into the firing chamber and aimed it at the thin-faced marauder for the third time. The shell misfired and a dirty-mouthing Charlie dropped his rifle and yanked out his pistol and blazed away at the dust-raising marauders, knowing that he hadn't a snowball's chance in hell of hitting them but it was a message telling them that he was still out for blood if they felt like riding back and continuing the fight.

Charlie came out into the open satisfied that the marauders had decided to cut their losses and had definitely gone. For how long he wouldn't like to guess. They weren't forgiving men. They would be back to get what the Good Book states, 'an eye for an eye, a tooth for a tooth'. They would also want blood, his, but that didn't bother him. Once he got things sorted out here he would be moving on to carry out his spying mission.

Charlie grabbed the dead marauder by the heels and dragged him out of the fire, kicking dirt on the flames that were still licking at the pieces of smouldering cloth that had once been the marauder's clothes. Charlie's jawed tightened as he turned the corpse on to its back.

Caleb Downes raised himself up on his elbows. 'He sure ain't a purty sight, pilgrim,' he said.

Charlie still gazing at the charred body answered him without turning his head.

'He sure ain't, that's the truth, mister. I've seen men on the receiving end of a cannon shell look prettier. Though as they say live tough, die tough.' Using his boot Charlie turned the body over on to its face. He didn't want the girl to black out again, this time with shock, then walked across to the elderly farmer.

'Thanks for your help, friend,' Caleb said. 'Is my daughter OK? I saw that sonuvabitch hit her but I can't even get over to see how she is because that bastard, toasted in the fire, plugged me in the leg. My name is Caleb Downes, friend, that's Liz.' Caleb nodded towards the girl.

'She'll be OK, Mr Downes,' Charlie said. 'Though I reckon she'll have a beaten prize-fighter's head when she wakes up. Seeing to your leg comes first, you've lost a heap of blood.' There was another reason why he had not gone over to the girl. Unshaven, covered in trail dust, clothes that had seen much better times, if she opened her eyes with him bending over her she would have thought that he was one of the marauders about to have his

64

pleasure with her. And then he would have an hysterical girl as well as a wounded old man on his hands.

Charlie cut Mr Downes' pants to examine the wound more closely. 'It's a good wound, Mr Downes, shell went straight through without splintering any bones. It will still need cleaning though.' Charlie smiled. 'I've a bottle of snake juice in my saddle-bag that's labelled whiskey. I was wondering what I could use it for; an Injun would turn up his nose at it if I offered him a drink of it. I'm Charlie Bannack from a long ways from this peaceful spot.'

Caleb smiled weakly back at him. 'I never expected a....'

'A Johnny Reb like me ridin' in to help you out,' interrupted Charlie. 'I could see that the odds were stacked against you, Mr Downes and being that I ain't a Johnny Reb no longer it seemed natural-like for one sodbuster to help another sodbuster out when he sees that he's got problems.'

'Yeah, well....' Caleb said. 'In any case if you hadn't showed up my place would have been destroyed for the second time and what could have happened to my daughter could have been a whole lot worse. I'm beholden to you, Mr Bannack.'

'There ain't no need to be, Mr Downes,' Charlie said. 'I opine you would have done the same for me if it had been me tryin' to hold off the raiders. That's enough of my gabbin', I'll go and get that whiskey....' Charlie's voice trailed away as he felt the cold, blood-chilling ring of a rifle muzzle pressing hard into his neck.

'Take your hands off my pa, you reb sonuvabitch or I'll send you to where you traitors belong—hell.' Liz's words came out as a painful close-lipped mumble.

Charlie slowly raised his hands skywards. He had underestimated the girl. She wasn't the fainting kind. He had no doubts that she meant her threat. He was as close to being killed as ever he had been during the war.

Liz had regained consciousness, still tasting blood in her mouth. The right side of her face was one dull, throbbing pain and a puffed-up cheek partially closed her eye, blurring her vision. Yet clear enough to see a man wearing a reb tunic bending over her pa. Oblivious to the dead man lying alongside her Liz gripped the wagon wheel and pulled herself on to her feet. She reached into the wagon and picked up the rifle and shakily, as cat-footed as she could, she crept across to the reb. Wincing softly with every step she took.

'Put the rifle down, Liz,' Caleb said. 'Mr Bannack here is a friend. Who do you think chased the marauders off? Killed two of 'em!'

Liz saw the blackened corpse by the fire, caught the sickly smell of scorched human flesh. Dropping the rifle she swung away from Charlie and noisily threw up. Charlie stood up and held her bowed shoulders till she had stopped her retching. Liz straightened up to turn and face him. She was too distraught to fully accept what her father had said and Charlie saw in the look she was giving him her inner doubts about just where his loyalties lay.

Charlie on his part saw a defiant-eyed, blood-drained face, one side marred by an ugly greenish bruise, framed by long raven-black hair, once held back from her face by the blue ribbon that now dangled loosely down her back. Charlie was no expert in the finer points of a woman's face and figure that turned her from being pretty into a real beauty. He was a man who liked what he liked. And he liked Miss Liz Downes. Dressed in her hoedown dance-dress, face back to normal, she would be the main attraction in the barn.

'OK, now?' he asked.

Liz nodded. She drew a cloth out of her pants pocket and wiped her mouth and face. 'I'll see to pa now.'

Miss Downes had another plus in her favour according to Charlie's weighing up of the fair sex. She had taken what she had been through like a man, no screaming fits, no crying jags, and was still capable of seeing to her wounded pa in spite of the pain she must be suffering from her swollen face. Miss Downes had true grit. He was only sorry he hadn't killed the sonuvabitch who had inflicted the pain on her. If he bumped into him again he wouldn't miss the chance of sending him to hell for sure.

Charlie buried the two dead marauders and turned their horses loose. When he returned to the shack Miss Downes had finished dressing her father's wound and Charlie could smell the welcome aroma of freshly brewed coffee. He grunted with satisfaction. Miss Liz Downes was OK, there was no doubt about it.

'Would you care for some coffee, Mr Bannack,' Liz said. 'Pa told me your name.'

Charlie noticed that Miss Downes' good eye was still regarding him suspiciously in spite of her offering him a cup of coffee. Charlie charitably forgave her for thinking bad thoughts about him. Men wearing reb uniforms had caused her and her pa a lot of grief. Charlie asked how her pa was.

'He's OK,' Liz said. 'I've stopped the bleeding but I'd like a regular doctor to have a look at it.' She managed a tortured looking smile as she handed Charlie back his bottle of whiskey. 'Pa took some, for medicinal purposes, or so he said.'

Charlie felt her pain with her, 'Miss Downes,' he said, 'I don't know whether or not you are against the partaking of strong liquor but it won't do you any harm for you to do likewise. Help to ease the pain somewhat.' Before she could say otherwise Charlie poured a measure into her cup. Charlie ached to tell her that she and her pa, if they hadn't already decided to, should pull out and head back to Kansas City, or wherever, before the marauders returned. He opined that it wasn't none of his business. Even if it was, Miss Liz Downes had a stubborn, ornery set to her jaw that gave Charlie the feeling that she wouldn't take kindly to anyone telling her what she should do if it went against her way of thinking. Advice from a Johnny Reb wouldn't get through to her at all.

Over the rim of her cup and all-mixed-up-inside Liz gave Mr Bannack quick but assaying glances. She would never have dreamed, even as short a time as a half-hour ago, that she would be drinking coffee with a hated reb, and sharing his damn liquor. Of course, Liz thought, Mr Bannack wasn't like the rebs who had killed her ma and her brothers. They had been of the same breed of scum that Mr Bannack had driven off. Mean-eyed, cruel-faced killers. Mr Bannack, in spite of her prejudged view of rebs in general, didn't look like that at all. He had beneath his beard a wide-open, country-boy's face. Older looking and more lined than his age, she reckoned. That would be the war. Union boys she had met who had been in the fighting had the same old-before-their-time looks. And reb or not he had come to the rescue of her and her pa at risk to his own life. No man had been willing to have even a fist fight at some dance on her behalf before.

Liz, for seemingly no apparent reason, felt the awakening inside her of a natural desire, long since suppressed, that set her blood racing throughout the whole of her body. Was she being physically attracted to Mr Bannack, a reb? Liz lowered her gaze in case Mr Bannack could read her feelings. Of course, she told herself, it could be the effects of the liquor he had tipped in her coffee that had stimulated her body. She didn't really think so. And that worried Liz. It was something she couldn't control. The last thing she wanted was to go all goosey over a reb. She had too much to do, look after Pa, and build up the farm, to even consider letting a Union boy spark up to her. Liz laid her cup, still half full, down on the ground on the off chance that it had been the strong liquor firing her blood and stopped her eyeballing of Mr Bannack.

'I take it that you'll be driftin' on, Mr Bannack,' Caleb said. 'If you're intendin' crossing the border you watch out for those three fellas you drove off. They're holed-up somewhere in Clay County.'

Charlie thin-smiled. 'With both eyes, Mr Downes. I ain't come through the war unharmed just to get myself backshot by a bunch of brush boys who don't accept that the war's over.'

'Mr Bannack,' Caleb said, his face boning over. 'Those boys were doin' their killin' and burnin' long ways before the war started. They burnt my place down, killed Ma and Liz's two brother, the murderin' sonsuvbitches. I wanted to do what you're doin', Mr Bannack, move on. Sell up and get to hell out of this valley.' Caleb's face softened somewhat. 'But Liz there, is as stubborn as her Ma was and won't let me sell. We came back to rebuild the old place up, foolishly thinkin' that the war had ended and you know the rest, Mr Bannack. I reckon that even Liz knows that me and her can't hold out against that kind of trouble on our own. So it seems that selling time has come round again.'

'Is someone willing to buy the place from you, Mr Downes?' a curious Charlie asked. 'Knowing that the Missouri raiders are still up to their old tricks? I saw all the deserted farms as I rode along the trail. I sort of reckoned they'd all been abandoned, owners killed in the war, or had their bellies full of bustin' the sods.'

'No, they're not abandoned, Mr Bannack,' replied Caleb. 'They belong now to Mr Lindford, a big man in the territory; his place is about forty miles due west of here. Bought the land cheap when their owners were driven off by all the raidin' that went on around here durin', and before, the war. He got raided like the rest of us but the proud sonuvabitch nailed the Union flag to his chimney stack daring the brush boys to come and do their worst, face him like real fightin' men. Yeah, Mr Lindford is a real Union man, could be our next State governor.'

Charlie noticed Miss Liz Downes' good eye sparking fire. He sympathized with her unsaid thoughts having the natural sour opinion of a farmer against a would-be land baron taking advantage of some poor sodbuster's misfortune. And Mr Downes' fervent support for Lindford didn't lay any of Charlie's doubts that, Mr 'All for the Union' Lindford, boldly baring his ass at the marauders, was a land-grabbing son-of-a-bitch. Getting hold of land cheap during the war and now hiring men, like the scum he had chased off, so that he could still buy it cheap. It was just a gut feeling but Liz Downes' derisive sniff

74

after her pa had finished speaking helped to confirm that feeling. He could scout around to see if he could pick up any more than rumours or talk relating to Lindford's land buying deals and pass it on to Lars Jackson. Whether it would be Secret Service business Charlie couldn't tell but it could help the Downes and the other farmers still working their land in the valley.

'All Mr Lindford suffered was a few burnt-down barns, Mr Bannack,' Liz said, her good eye still glinting as if daring Charlie or her pa to doubt her sayso. 'This piece of land is one piece Mr Lindford isn't going to get. Even if we can't get on it to live peaceful-like till I'm old and grey-haired.' Still angry-voiced she said, 'I'd be obliged, Mr Bannack, if you would help me to get pa on to the wagon then we can make the trip to the doctor at Palmers Flats.'

Charlie had been asked in more kindlier ways for his help though his smile didn't show his own anger. Liz Downes was under great stress and he opined she was entitled to sound a mite ornery. 'It will be a pleasure, Miss Downes,' he said. 'And I'll ride with you till you get to Palmers Flats.'

Liz was angry with her pa for wanting to sell the land, angry with herself for thinking good, blood-warming thoughts about Mr Bannack and it all came out in a blurted, 'There's no need to put yourself out for us any further, reb!'

Charlie's face stoned over in righteous anger. He hadn't wanted Miss Liz Downes to throw her arms around his neck in gratitude for saving her from being raped, though that would have been very rewarding, he thought, but throwing dirt in his face riled him. It was time that the young spitfire understood that the war was over, that she forgot the past. There were no rebels now. The marauders weren't rebs, just mean murdering assholes. Doing what they did not for a cause, lost or otherwise, but as a way of life. With a voice as hard as his face he grated, 'If I hadn't put myself out a short while back I reckon you know what would have happened to you. If you and your pa are unfortunate enough to meet the same bunch on the trail to Palmers Flats you'll damn well know what they'll do to you. Is your stubborn pride worth that, Miss Downes?' Charlie's face muscles eased a little. 'Get that chip off your shoulder and show a little Christian forgiveness to us born-again Unionists.'

Liz felt herself go all hot again, this time with embarrassed shame and found she couldn't hold Mr Bannack's accusing gaze. If the marauders did catch up with her and her pa, Liz gave a shudder of icy fear. Stubborn pride couldn't be weighed against the outcome of that meeting. Mr Bannack was right, and she had been wrong to talk to him the way she had; the war was over. But old hates like old love die hard and she still couldn't face the man she had still branded as a reb, though soft-voiced, she said, 'Me and my pa will be most grateful if you rode along with us, Mr Bannack. Though I'm not too happy about you probably having to risk your life again on our behalf.'

Then, as suddenly and as unexpected as

her earlier warm feelings towards Charlie, the reaction of what she had been through, and how much worse it could have turned out, Liz burst into tears. Washing away the last of her anger and hate. When she raised her head to look at Charlie he saw only tears and pain in her eyes.

Inwardly smiling Charlie drew her close to him, Liz not hindering him at all, feeling the warm softness of her body pressing into him. He felt six feet tall, thinking that he would go out of his way to seek out the son-of-a-bitch who had used his fist on her and finish him off for keeps. Being the President's man would have to hang-fire and to hell with what Mr Lars Jackson would say.

'You get it out of your system, Miss Liz,' he said soothingly. 'It ain't been a picnic you've just had.' and he held Liz just that little tighter as she sobbed her fears and anxieties away on his shoulder.

'Ain't you goin' to take me to Palmers Flats, daughter?' Caleb Downes growled mock-angrily. 'Or are you just goin' to let me sit here and bleed to death?'

Reluctantly, or so Charlie thought, Liz eased herself out of his grasp shy-smiling up at him. There and then Charlie made a solemn promise that if ever he got out of this hole he had been pushed into he would come back here and help Caleb Downes build up his house, and pay courtship to Miss Liz Downes. If she didn't object to a broke-to-the-wide, ragged-assed, ex-reb sparking her up.

FIVE

Mason sat on the porch of a splayed, sun-bleached planked shack in the timber and brush country east of Little Creek, Missouri, nursing his wounded shoulder. His face was set in an agonized scowl, trying to ease the pain of his wound by heaping death wishes, each one more bloodthirsty than the next, on the unknown bushwhacker who had driven them off the Downes' place, plugged him, and killed Slim and Bubba—the scowl became fiercer—and stopped him from having his pleasure with that pretty young bitch.

He had banked on clearing out the last of the sodbusters along the border in a series of swift, hard-hitting raids then he and the boys would be paid the balance of their due and haul-ass out of Clay County. Ride south to the Nations, m'be Texas. It was getting too dangerous for

80

him to operate in the border territory. The blue-belly authorities, now they hadn't a war to fight, had concentrated their efforts on clearing Missouri of the last of the reb guerilla bands. Quantrill and 'Bloody' Bill Anderson and their boys were either dead or in prison. The other raiders were being hunted down by blue-belly horse soldiers. The Mason gang—Mason spat in the dust, his face a devil's mask, or what was left of it—were the only raiders still running free in western Missouri. Mason knew that some day the blue bellies would stumble across their hole-up in these woods and come in strength and root them out.

There were still men in the territory, loners, refusing the amnesty the Unionists were offering all former brush boys if they came in with their hands held high. But even they were getting the message that it wasn't good for their health to stay in this section of Missouri. It would prove difficult to make up for the loss of Slim and Bubba. His busted shoulder made it impossible for him to partake in any raiding, that made the gang three short. Down to two, Andy and Dave. Mason vented his spleen by raising the dust at his feet with another spurt of chaw-juice. No matter how he looked at it two men didn't make a gang however wild-assed they were. They'd be hard pressed to raid a dry goods store with a blind clerk behind the counter let alone take on the snap-shooting bastard who had plugged him.

He didn't want a big gang; it wasn't necessary to be riding at the head of a small army of men to do the job he had been paid to do. More men meant that the payment had to be spread around that much thinner. Andy and Dave were in Little Creek seeking out a couple of likely recruits to the Mason gang. In spite of the pain he was suffering Mason smiled, a fearsome grin that matched his devil's mask face. When the raiding was over they would meet up with an accident, a fatal one. He reckoned that 'Johnny-come-latelies' to the gang weren't entitled to a share of the pot. Especially when they had missed out on the shooting at the Downes' place.

Charlie rode slowly along the dry-rutted track that passed for Main street, Little Creek. Past two stores, an eating-house, a livery barn, all fronting one side of the street, and drew up outside a ramshackled, double-storeyed building with half-a-dozen horses tied to a rail outside it. Most of the painted legend across the front of the building had faded with age and the weather but Charlie managed to pick out the last few letters of the word, saloon. He dismounted, tied his horse to the rail, then drew out his rifle. Face twisted in a real stomping man's fish-eyed look he strode into the saloon. Once more the President's man, ears flapping for any talk about threats against the man he had sworn an oath to protect.

He had left Liz and her pa at Palmers Flats, waiting till the old man had his wound seen to by the local doc and passed as OK and Liz had had treatment to ease the pain in her face and bring the swelling down. He had close-eyed Liz and spoke to her as though they had been closely

83

acquainted all their lives.

'You ain't thinkin' foolish thoughts about going back to the farm, Miss Liz,' he said.

It was a direct-gazing Liz that answered him. 'No, Mr Bannack, I'm not. We're staying here in Palmers Flats with kin of course.' Then the fire came into her voice again. 'But that don't mean I'm going to let pa sell our land to Mr Lindford.'

Charlie grinned. 'I never thought you would, Miss Liz. You and your pa just hang on in. The trouble you've been getting won't last much longer, believe me. Law is coming to the border country.' Charlie's grin broadened. 'M'be only blue-belly law but it will put paid to the raidin' for good.'

Liz smiled back at him. 'Are you riding back this way again from wherever you're heading to, Mr Bannack?'

'I had it in my mind to swing this way again if everything comes out OK for me,' Charlie said.

Liz sweet-smiled at him. 'I'll look out for you then, Charlie,' and reaching up on

84

her toes she kissed the surprised Charlie full on the mouth.

After the still moon-faced, smiling Charlie had mounted up and ridden out of Palmers Flats, Liz, standing watching him go, got to wondering why it was she was having such deep, blood-warming thoughts about a man she had only known for a few hours. And a hated Johnny Reb at that. Much deeper than the natural good feelings for a man who had saved her from being raped. Her liking for Mr Bannack didn't make any sense. She knew absolutely nothing whatever about him. He was older than her, could be married with a family. Then there was his, 'If things went well for him'. What on earth did that mean? Was he also a marauder? A man with a price on his head? Liz finally opined that it was no use getting herself even more confused than she was right now thinking that m'be she could have a closer, friendlier relationship with Mr Bannack for, more than likely, she would never see him again, though she surely hoped that she would. He had said that he was coming back and he had no reason to lie to her. On that hope she watched his trail-dust drift away praying that all would go well for Mr Bannack.

There were over a dozen drinkers in the saloon, more than Charlie expected this early in the day. He put it down to the fact that men who had returned from the war hadn't settled down to the normal routine of peaceful living again. He sure hadn't and look where it had got him. Two of the saloon's customers were standing at the bar, the rest were sitting at tables playing cards or soft-talking. The inside of the saloon, its fly-blown mirrors, kicked and scuffed bar, plaster peeling walls, had the same time-passed-by look as the rest of Little Creek. The war had aged everything.

Charlie gave the customers a sweeping, kiss-my-ass glare as he walked across to the bar, clattering his rifle down on it as he bellied up to the counter. 'Whiskey!' he snapped at the barkeep idly polishing glasses at the other end of the bar. Through the bar mirror he noticed that the two drinkers at the same end as the barkeep was, an Indian-faced pair, were eyeing him. Charlie thought of giving them a 'drop-dead' look back but he didn't want to overplay his part. The two had the cut of men who wouldn't take kindly to being needled and it could end up in a gunfight. He wanted to create an impression as a disgruntled reb still wanting to fight on, not as an up-and-coming pistollero. Men in this part of the territory were still trigger-happy and being no fast-draw kid he could get himself killed. That wouldn't help any in keeping President Johnson safe from meeting the same fate as Abe Lincoln or enable him to keep his promise to Miss Liz Downes.

The barkeep, a purple, prominent-veined nosed old man came shuffling along the bar with a bottle of whiskey and, with hope in his heart, two glasses. He ran his tongue over craving-lips like a hungry hound smelling the nearness of its next meal as his latest customer filled his glass with a generous measure of liquor. Charlie picked up his glass and downed the drink in one effortless gulp then poured himself another four fingers. Seeing the hound dog-like pleading in the barkeep's eyes he filled the extra glass.

'Have one on me, old-timer,' he said. 'And drink to the health of General George Pickett who led us Virginians against the blue-belly sonsuvbitches hunkered down along Cemetery Ridge. The old butcher sent us cheering into hell, old-timer, left more than half of the boys lying in the cornfield and on the ridge. But by heck if Robert E. Lee hadn't told us to quit I would have fought the Unionists till hell froze over then fought them on the ice.' Charlie beady-eyed the barkeep. 'And that ain't this burro's piss you're passin' off as whiskey in this dog-shit town talkin', old-timer, it's the gospel truth, so help me.' Charlie switched his gaze on to the two men further along the bar. Favouring them with an all-tooth smile he said, 'Would you care to join me in the toasting of some brave boys, gents?'

It hadn't been a wild guess by Charlie opining that the men were ex-rebs. The pistols and holsters belted across their middles were Confederate army issue. That the pair, if they still harboured a grievance against the victorious Union, could be a lead in the hunt for Mr Lars Jackson's mysterious M he wouldn't care to hazard a guess. But he had to start his spying somewhere. Charlie had no idea that no more than a few hours ago he was trying to kill the two of them. A man firing and being fired on has very little time to get a good clear picture of the man framed in the sights of his rifle.

Andy grinned and elbowed Dave in the ribs. 'That loud-mouthed asshole looks like one of the boys Mason asked us to find,' he whispered. Raising his voice he said, 'Me and my pard here, mister, will be dee-lighted to drink with a man who fought at Gettysburg.'

Andy and Dave introduced themselves, saying that they were former rebs, guerilla raiders in this section of the territory. That information caused Charlie to think that at least if he couldn't help the President he could m'be help Liz Downes and her pa. When the whiskey took hold of the pair he'd pump them, find out if they knew of any guerillas who were still operating along the border as though the war hadn't ended. Not too pressingly, he opined, for the pair for all their smiles and back-slapping had eyes that didn't mirror their apparent good humour. They were natural-born suspicious-minded men.

Another two men on hearing that Charlie had fought at Gettysburg got up from a nearby table and joined him at the bar. 'I'm Mel Broughton,' the taller of the two said. 'This is my brother, Zeb. Our regiment fought alongside you Virginians at Gettysburg.'

'Let's go back to your table, boys, and drink in comfort,' Charlie said magnanimously. 'Any sonuvabitch who fireballed up that ridge and came through in one piece is entitled to get roarin' drunk once in a while.'

The barkeep cursed, his source of free drinks had dried up. He almost wished that he'd fought at Gettysburg, or at any other Goddamned battle so that he could have continued with the drinking. He would drink with the Devil, if he paid for the liquor.

By the time the third bottle had been emptied—Charlie, not being a drinking man, couldn't remember whether or not it was three or four they had downed—Dave dropped the broad hint that men who had no taste for being called losers could still fight for the Cause across the border in Kansas.

'It'll be work you boys know how to handle,' he said, narrow-eyeing Charlie and the Broughtons for their reactions to his proposal. 'And a heap better paid and nowhere as ass-pinchin' as fireballin' up Cemetery Ridge.' Dave gave a fang-toothed smile. 'All it is is chasin' a few Nigra-lovin' sodbusters off their land. Should take no sweat at all.' Dave, the smile still fixed on his face, neglected to tell them that if they met up with the rifleman who had done for Slim and Bubba it wouldn't be sweat they'd be losing. 'Of course,' he added, 'the boss will have to OK it first.'

The Broughton brothers looked at each

other before speaking. 'Me and Mel's in,' Zeb said. 'We ain't goin' back to walkin' behind a plough gazin' at a mule's ass agin.'

All eyes focused on Charlie. He glared back at them, all hard-assed and fiery. 'The war ain't over for me just because a played-out old man signed some piece of paper sayin' that I had to stop shootin' at blue bellies.' He splashed more whiskey into his glass, hoping that his fellow drinkers would think that his shaking hand was the whiskey working not the fear he was feeling. They was no need to sound out Dave and Andy about men who could be harassing the Kansas farmers, he had joined their gang, committed to carrying out their leader's orders or he would be as dead as all the boys they had been talking about. All there was about spying, Lars Jackson had said, was to keep your ears open and listen good. The Yankee son-of-a-bitch didn't tell him it would be damn dangerous as well.

'We swing left here, boys,' Dave said and

Mel pulled his horse off the trail to let the four of them pass by him to ride along a trail that was no wider than a goat-track, then dropping in behind them, effectively blocking the escape route of any of the new recruits to the gang should they want out at this late stage. Charlie was still too drunk to put his mind to work out some plan so to give his brain a rest he thought he would wait till he knew the full strength of the gang and where they were holed-up, reason telling him to let himself be carried along with the situation and hope for a break coming his way. A miracle more likely, Charlie thought morosely.

The track suddenly came out of the trees, opening up into a wide clearing with a creek running through it. On the nearside bank was an old shack with a man standing on the stoop eyeing their approach. Charlie noticed that the man had his right arm resting in a sling across his chest, and a pistol held down by his left leg. He sobered up fast. The last time he had seen that mean-eyed face it had been framed in the sights of his repeater. He had hit the jackpot, but as yet couldn't get his hands on it. Easy, careful, was the way he had to work from now on in or he wouldn't be around to collect his prize, the plugging of the man who had harmed Miss Liz Downes.

They drew up alongside the shack, Andy and Dave dismounting, Charlie and the Broughton boys waiting till the man who was weighing them up said, curtly, 'Step down and come inside.' Charlie followed him into the shack, somewhat cheered up by seeing the pain-twisted face of the man he had wounded, and for guessing right that he was the boss.

'I'm Mason,' Mason said. 'The man who gives the orders around here.'

Charlie and the Tennessee boys were sitting on empty crates at a table that swayed and creaked every time they rested their arms on it. Mason hard-eyed them as though he was trying to read their innermost thoughts. A bottle of whiskey and glasses were on the table but unlike the Broughtons, Charlie didn't touch it. Easy and careful also meant sober. So far things were going OK for him, Mason not doubting who he said he was.

'If you boys can't stomach that,' Mason continued. 'Then you can ride on out of here, with no hard feelin's from me.'

Mason grinned, all brotherly love. Charlie knew it was as false as his telling him they could leave after being shown the gang's hideout. Andy and Dave, standing behind them, would shoot down any of them who made for the door.

Putting on a show of anger Charlie snarled, 'It ain't the first time I've took orders. If I hadn't wanted to join up with you I would have stayed back there in Little Creek drinking with that old barkeep.'

Mason gave him another close-eyeballing before saying, 'OK kid, you're in.' Then he switched his gaze on to the Broughtons.

'Boss,' said Zeb, 'if the price was right me and Mel would plug our own grey-haired old pappy. Ain't that the truth, Brother?' Both of them broke into a fit of high-pitched womanish laughter.

In spite of their mirth Charlie didn't

think that Zeb was kidding. Zeb and Mel were born marauders, kill without mercy. It was going to be one against five if he ever got the chance to make his play.

Mason got to his feet. 'That's settled then, boys. See to your horses; Dave will show you where to bed them down. You can sleep in the shack here, bedrolls on the floor. Grub's only sowbelly and beans and coffee but I reckon men that's fought their way up Cemetery Ridge are used to rough livin'.' Mason favoured them with another one of his smiles. Charlie had seen rattlers wearing more heart-warming grins.

Lars Jackson, tending bar in the Plains saloon, was no nearer to discovering who Mr M was than he had been in Washington the first time he'd read M's letter to John Wilkes Booth. Proving what he'd known all along that his trip to Kansas City would be a waste of time. The names bandied about by the drinkers on the other side of the bar of men who, or could be, involved in the assassination plot ranged from Jefferson Davis, General Robert E. Lee, and every other ex-reb in the South.

He couldn't see the inexperienced Charlie Bannack having any more success than he was having. Unkindly selling Charlie short, Lars pictured him rib-kicking his horse somewhere between Kansas City and the Mexican border, giving up on being one of the President's men.

SIX

Charlie and the Broughton brothers crossed into Kansas to earn their keep as members of Mason's gang of marauders.

'There's only a young girl and an old man on the farm,' Mason had told them. 'You'll have no trouble at all in putting the shits up the old sodbuster and make him want to quit his land.' He neglected to tell them that they were acting as Judas-goats. If they got the same hot reception he'd got he could always hire some more bird-brained country boys and make different plans to get Downes off his property.

Charlie grinned to himself. I sure won't have the trouble you met there, you lying bastard, he thought. Mel and Zeb might if things went his way. Innocently he asked Mason how the Southern cause could be kept alive by throwing an old man and a girl off their land. Raiding Yankee banks

98

and holding up their trains he could savvy. It would make headline-news. The whole South would read about it.

Mason gave him a sharp-eyed look. 'That's the way the man who pays us wants it, kid. And that's the way it's gonna be, understand?'

Charlie nodded 'Understood, boss. I was just wonderin', that's all.'

'You don't do any wonderin', or thinkin',' Mason growled. 'That's my job.'

Charlie thought that it would give him great pleasure when the opportunity came to ventilate Mason's hide with Colt shells. He grinned broadly at the thought. 'You're the boss, boss.'

Mason, totally misreading the reason for Charlie's grin, ceased close-eyeing him. 'As long as you don't forget it, kid, you'll be OK.'

Knowing that they were riding to a deserted farm allowed Charlie to relax and assay the Broughtons, guessing how fast their reactions would be if he ever had to face them. More importantly, how fast could he be? Charlie didn't claim to be a shootist, a fast cool hand with a gun. In the war it had been different. A man's blood gets pounding fast and hot in battle, makes him do wild crazy things like walking through cannon-fire to storm a picket fence or a wall lined with Union sharpshooters. Driven forward by bravery or fear it didn't matter. A man walking shoulder to shoulder with his buddies couldn't let them down by turning tail. Facing two men, cold-bloodedly, sent shivers down Charlie's spine as brave as he had proved he was. Dave and Andy would be no easy meat. M'be, he thought hopefully, if he could down Mason the gang would break up and stop the raiding, bringing peace to the border country at last. That's if he could get Mason to face him one to one.

Zeb's, 'We're must be gettin' close to the Downes' place, Mel. There's the black-faced butte Mason said we'd see before we dropped down on to the farm,' brought Charlie back to the present. And a bloody confrontation with the Broughton brothers sooner than he expected or prepared for.

Before they crested the ridge Mel, pointing along to his left, cried, 'Well lookee there, Zeb, a real live female. Let's go and pay her a call, show her how warm-blooded and lovin' we Tennessee boys are.'

Charlie saw the lone figure of a girl some distance away who, although she was wearing a dress now, he knew could only be Liz. Charlie cursed as the realization screwed his stomach up into a sickening knot. What the hell was she doing here when she had faithfully promised him to stay with her pa in Palmers Flats?

'Remember, Mel,' laughed Zeb, his face working in anticipation of the pleasures he was intending to partake in. 'I'm the eldest and I'm claimin' first taste of her!'

Heels were dug savagely in horses' flanks and both brothers, whooping and howling like bronco Kiowa, galloped along the ridge to their unexpected, tasty windfall. A stone-faced Charlie followed in their tracks.

Liz's quiet moments of meditation, as she gazed at her ma's and brothers' graves in the small burial plot ringed by a whitewashed picket fence, thinking of things as they had been when they had first came into the valley, was brutally shattered by the sound of yelling and the drumming of horses' hooves. Wide-eyed she swung round and saw two riders closing in her. They pulled up near enough for Liz to feel and smell the body heat of their horses and to force her back against the fence. Close enough for her to see the riders' leering, wanting looks. Her alarm turned to abject fear, her hand flying to her mouth in an attempt to stifle her cry of terror. God, she sobbed silently, this time there was no Mr Bannack to help her.

'We ain't goin' to hurt you, missee,' Mel said. 'Not if you're real nice and friendly to me and my brother.'

Liz felt the fence sway behind her as she pressed harder against it as if somehow it was able to protect her from the terrible things the marauders would do to her. Suddenly her fears lifted, a third rider had drawn up behind the man who had spoken to her. Mr Bannack. Her prayers had been answered. Just as suddenly her welcoming smile froze and her fears came flooding back. The men who wanted to use her were marauders and Mr Bannack was riding with them. Had he saved her from rape the first time so that later he could take her when she was on her own, away from her pa? And she had foolishly allowed herself to think that she was falling in love with him. Yet part of her still wanted to believe that her opinion of Mr Bannack had been right; how else could she have been attracted to him? But her eyes couldn't lie, he was with the marauders. Managing a weak smile Liz straightened up from the fence and sounding braver than she really was she said, 'I didn't think I'd see you again so soon, Mr Bannack.'

Mel screwed round in his saddle, clawing for his pistol. 'Something smells here, Zeb, this pilgrim knowin' the Unionist bitch!'

Charlie, his pistol already fisted, shot Mel between the eyes. The close-range shot cleared Mel off his horse, the top of his head a splintered-bone, red mess.

Charlie thumbed back the hammer of the Colt and brought it across his chest and fired at Zeb. It was too panicky-quick to be a killing shot and only winged Zeb. As Charlie cocked his pistol for another shot he knew with the clear-sightedness of a man looking at death in the eye if he hadn't caught the brothers off-guard it would have been him not Mel lying there with half his head blown away.

He triggered off a load a split-second before Zeb's pistol lined up on him. Zeb screeched like a badly wounded horse as the shell tore into his stomach, doubling him up over his saddle before slipping off and falling to the ground. Rolling and twisting, heels kicking dirt Zeb was dying hard and painful. An Indian-faced Charlie stood up in his stirrups and, as a man might do to put a horse with a broken leg out of its misery, he fired a single shot at Zeb and both brothers were on their way to hell. It was only then Charlie felt a burning sensation on his right temple and felt the warm trickle of blood running down his cheek and realized that Zeb had fired a shot he'd neither seen nor heard. He'd been luckier than he'd thought. He dropped back into his saddle and sheathed his pistol, his hands too unsteady to reload it.

An all ragged-nerved Charlie looked at a slack-jawed, ashen-faced Liz. 'You little fool!' he blurted out. 'I told you to stay with your pa in Palmers Flats! Do you want to be raped? Do you have a fancy to see men shot down on your behalf? Do you damn well want to see me dead?'

Liz's face stiffened in anger at Charlie's outburst. Matching his glare she yelled, 'I said I wouldn't go back to the farm, Mr Bannack, and I haven't! I came here to tend Ma's and....' Charlie's wild-eyed, blood-streaked face tore at her insides and no longer could she fight him. Not when she knew she was in the wrong coming out here on her own and had almost got the man she intended to marry some day, killed. She turned away from Charlie, to look over at the graves, sobbing uncontrollably.

Charlie saw her shoulders heaving and

his anger vanished. 'Charlie,' he said under his breath, 'you're one first-class asshole. The kid's gone through enough without you ranting at her like an hysterical old woman.' He dismounted and walked over to her and putting his hands on her shoulders gently turned her towards him. Smiling he said, 'You'll have to stop all this cryin' everytime we meet. It's got me thinkin' that you don't like me.'

'OK, Mr Bannack,' Liz said. 'I almost got you killed.' She put her arms around Charlie and pressed closer to him, and the tears flowed again.

'No, you didn't,' replied Charlie. 'It was on the cards that I would have had to face those two sometime. You brought that time a mite earlier that's all. And gave me the edge.'

'But you're wounded, Mr Bannack,' Liz said, drawing back and lightly touching the bullet graze on Charlie's head.

'Ain't nothing but a scratch, Miss Liz,' Charlie said, thinking that if he suffered no worse injuries by the time Mr Lars Jackson called it a day and went back to Washington and left him free to pay court to Liz Downes he would be highly delighted. Reluctantly he eased the warm, sweet-smelling Miss Downes away from him. 'You do what you came to do, Miss Liz,' he said. 'I'll do what I've got to do.'

Charlie helped Liz on to the wagon then handed her the reins. 'You'll meet no trouble on the trail to Palmers Flats, Miss Liz,' he told her. 'But don't risk coming out again; there's still some of the gang raidin' this side of the border and I mightn't be able to show up when needed. And your ma wouldn't like you to get killed on her behalf, would she?'

'I'll stay with my pa, Mr Bannack, I promise. If, on your solemn oath, you promise me that you'll get that wound seen to when you get where you're heading for. I really don't know why you won't let me clean it up for you now.'

Charlie grinned. 'I'm keeping it like this to impress a certain assho....beggin' your pardon, Miss Liz, a certain fella in

Missouri. I've got to convince him that what happened here didn't happen that way at all.'

Liz, not wishing to hear what business Mr Bannack was involved in in case it set her worrying more than he was now about his safety stopped the talking by bending down and kissing Charlie full on the lips, a long, lover's kiss. Before Charlie came back down to earth Liz had jerked at the reins and the wagon was rolling along the trail. Over her shoulder she cried, 'Next time we meet I hope it's Liz and Charlie, not this high-falutin' Miss Liz and Mr Bannack!'

'As long as you ain't calling me the late Charlie Bannack,' Charlie muttered gloomily as he walked to his horse. The Broughton brothers were wrapped in their blankets and strapped across their horses, the horses linked together by a rope. Charlie mounted up and took hold of Zeb's horse's reins. 'OK, my four-legged friend,' he said. 'Let's go and let Mr Mason know that he has to go out recruiting again.'

A glowering Mason watched Charlie and

the macabre load he was leading ride up to the shack. 'What the hell's happened, Bannack?' he growled, after giving the dead men no more than a cursory glance.

Charlie dismounted and favoured Mason with a hard-faced scowl of his own. 'See this,' he said, putting a finger on his head wound, 'A hair's breadth closer and I'd be stretched face down across my horse. And you said that there was only an old man and a girl on the farm. It sure wasn't them that plugged the boys there and laid a slug across my head. I seen the sonuvabitch who did the shooting, a big, mean-looking fella, when he came out of the trees to see if he'd done for us all. He was toting a rifle and wore a lawman's badge. I lay doggo, crapping myself till he went back in the trees. I got on to my feet then, hoping I'd get a shot at him but I heard him ride off.'

Charlie kept up the hard-eyeing. 'I can take being shot at, Mason, as long as I know that there's a chance I might get thrown down on but I don't take kindly to walking like a greenhorn dude into some bushwhacker's gun sights.' To play out his bluff to the full Charlie let his hand drop to the butt of his pistol. 'If that's the way you operate I want out.' His angry stare daring Mason to draw on him.

Mason knew that he had been pushed into a tight corner. The kid wouldn't take much more upsetting before he pulled out his pistol and shot holes in him. And he had no backup, Dave and Andy hadn't returned yet. Mason had a fleeting black thought that m'be they had met the same fate as the hillbillies then he would have no gang at all. With a busted shoulder he had no chance of beating the kid to a draw if the kid pushed it to a showdown. Forcing his face into a resemblance of a smile he said, lyingly, 'Take it easy, kid, I didn't know about this lawman. When Dave and Andy come in the four of us will ride into Palmers Flats and seek the sonuvabitch out. Then we'll try a little bushwhacking ourselves. You go inside and help yourself to the whiskey, I'll see to the horses. We can see the boys decently planted later.'

It was a wide-grinning Charlie who

poured out himself a drink. Things so far were running his way. Half the gang gone and he had given Mason something to keep him awake at nights, fretting over a non-existent lawman. And he had got himself a girl, well almost. There was Mason, Andy and Dave to be put out of circulation but that didn't dampen Charlie's reckoning of having done a good job. If he had known that Andy and Dave weren't at the shack when he had first ridden in he would have shot Mason there and then. It was too late now; Mason was on the alert watching his every move. He would have to wait for his next break to come along.

SEVEN

Silas Procter, Chief Field Agent of the western division of the Pinkerton National Detective Agency, casually noticed the tall, thin-faced man across Main Street and enter the Plains saloon. Suddenly the memory cells in his brain began to whirl. He had seen that face before somewhere and Procter, by profession, never forgot a face. Where, he couldn't rightly recollect for the moment. Had he been a former Pinkerton? Was his face decorating a wanted flyer? One thing was for sure, Procter thought, that man and his paths had crossed.

He followed the man into the saloon to study him at closer range, to m'be jog his annoying memory lapse into remembering just where the hell they had met. Procter was surprised to see that the man now wore a barkeep's apron and was taking up

112

his post behind the bar. For a moment he thought that he must have seen him tending bar in some other town but he didn't think so. His curiosity fully aroused Procter walked over to the bar and ordered a whiskey so that he could get a real close look at his memory jogger. The man served him then moved along the bar to see to another customer's needs. Procter smirked at himself in the bar mirror. He hadn't lost his touch. The face and where he had seen it clicked.

It had been during the latter part of the war before Grant's final attack against the Confederate forces entrenched around Richmond. The agency had been running a whole network of agents behind the reb lines and he and Mr Alan Pinkerton, the boss of the agency, were in Washington to brief the Army top brass about their assessment of the information the spies had gleaned about the Confederates' military capabilities and dispositions in front of Grant's army. Also at the briefing was President Lincoln, listening to all that Mr Pinkerton was relating to the generals.

After the report Lincoln thanked Mr Pinkerton and told him to pass on his good wishes and congratulations to the agents working behind the reb lines. When the President left the room, four men, civilian-dressed, left with him. His Secret Service bodyguards. One of them had just served him a drink.

Solving one mystery set Proctor a more intriguing one. What was a President's man doing in Kansas City? Retired from the service and working as a barkeep? Balls, Procter thought caustically. The only reason, he opined, big enough to bring a top Secret Service man all the way to Kansas City would be the ongoing investigation to root out and punish everyone who had been involved in the plot to kill old Abe. The Pinkerton Detective Agency had scores of agents following their own tip-offs and leads.

The Secret Service must have their hands on information the Pinkertons hadn't got. Not even Alan Pinkerton himself would believe that anyone in the Free-State of Kansas was linked in any way with the plotters. It irked Procter somewhat. He had thought that the agency and the Secret Service were running a double team on the case, passing on whatever information each of them picked up to each other. Naturally Procter didn't make his presence known to the Secret Service agent, not wanting to blow his cover.

He didn't think that rule applied later that night at his regular weekly poker game. The mayor, the local banker, the colonel from the fort and Mr Lindford were all men of honour and of the highest integrity, and solid Unionists to a man, used to hearing privileged information and keeping tight-lipped about it. The talk as the hands were being dealt out was how the new President was making out after living in the shadow of a giant like Abe Lincoln. Procter dropped in his piece of news, the spotting of a Secret Service agent tending bar in the Plains saloon.

'He can't be here to help to round up those Missouri outlaws, Frank and Jesse James,' he said. 'Thats regular law-enforcer's business, though the Pinkertons have been asked by the railroad people to help the lawmen out.' Procter favoured his fellow card-players with a cocksure grin. 'No, gentlemen, the only reason he could be in KC is that the Secret Service have a strong lead that someone here was a confederate of John Wilkes Booth.'

Lindford's Havana suddenly tasted like rolled horse-droppings. He hadn't had to guess why the Union agent was in town. Somehow he knew why. It was as if he had received a Western Union wire telling him so. John Wilkes Booth was reaching out from his grave to drag him down to keep him company. Lindford struggled to control his fears from showing and managed to act normally, playing four hands of poker, losing them all, much to the surprise and delight of the rest of the table, before pleading he had some urgent business to attend to and asked to be excused.

Out in the street, on his own, Lindford began to think more rationally, thinking like Thomas M. Lindford, landowner and future governor of Kansas. How the secret

Service had picked up information that Booth had links with someone in Kansas City didn't matter. He knew if Booth had mentioned his name before he died he would by now have suffered the same fate as the rest of the conspirators. He could only guess that Booth must have kept the letter he had sent to him, registered as having been posted in Kansas City. If it had been the letter they didn't seem to be making much headway with it. They weren't breathing down his neck. And he had heard no news or rumours to suggest otherwise. The lead wasn't really a lead at all. The letter could have been posted by someone passing through Kansas City. Still, as a gambling man he knew long odds occasionally come up. To make sure that they didn't come up this time the slim lead that the agent was checking out in Kansas City had to be stopped as from now, by killing the agent.

Getting Mason to gun the agent down in Kansas City, Lindford opined, was no solution. That action would raise suspicious eyebrows back in Washington, making them think that their man had got real close to what he had come to Kansas City to seek out and paid for it with his life. No, he thought, the agent would have to appear to have left town, following the lead some other place. Then the nosy son-of-a-bitch could be killed and his body hidden deep and good. After a while when their agent hadn't reported in, Washington would no doubt accept that he was dead. Lindford gave a cold, humourless smile, and who killed him and where, they would never discover even if they sent every agent they had south. And Lindford was confident, he would bet his life on it—in fact he was doing just that—Kansas City would be one place they wouldn't spend a lot of time making enquiries. Gus Freedman would have to make another trip across the border. And also impress on the wild-ass Mason, that the business had to be handled delicately.

Charlie, sitting on the shack's porch with Mason and Dave, saw Andy, acting as lookout, come into the clearing and call out, 'Rider comin' in, boss! The dude from Kansas!'

The little fat man gave Charlie a quick but shrewd glance as he stepped down from his horse in front of the shack, from beady eyes, thought Charlie, that didn't match his soft-faced, storeclerk appearance. A man, if events brought them face to face, wouldn't have to be underestimated. Dude he might look, but the inner killer-streak showed through the hard eyes every bit as vicious as Mason and his two boys. When Mason and the little dude had gone into the shack Charlie casually asked Dave if the dude was one of the gang. Dave gave him a hard, mind-your-own-business, glare. 'Nah,' he said. 'It's Mason's rich uncle,' and burst into laughter at his joke.

Charlie's insides hardened. When the time came to shoot lumps off Mason he would do likewise to the asshole sitting beside him and get the same amount of pleasure doing so. He reckoned that the little dude was the messenger boy, the fixer of whoever was doing the land-grabbing, and Charlie was certain that Lindford was the bossman. The bigger that man in the community the further away he would want to be from the men who were doing his dirty work.

There was no way he could back-trail the dude, Dave and Andy were watching him like hungry buzzards searching for a meal. Dave especially. He hadn't fully swallowed his tale of the killings at the farm; Mason had told the pair of them of the shooting dead of the Tennessee brothers. Dave had given him a lip-curling look and said, 'The marshal at Palmers Flats is a little wizened old goat; I've seen him, boss.'

Charlie could feel Mason's eyes boring into his back. It was no time to lose his nerve or it would be lead from Mason's pistol doing the boring into his hide. 'I don't know where he's marshal of,' he snarled in Dave's face, 'I was in no position to ask the sonuvabitch. But I do know he wasn't an old goat and he wore a lawman's badge. So if you're still doubting my sayso, well, step outside and we'll settle it with pistols. Me and the brothers rode into a bushwhacker's ambush and I ain't

120

about to stand here and let an asshole like you say otherwise.'

Charlie waited, nerves all screwed up, for Dave's reactions. He had pushed him into making his play or eat crow. If Dave did go for his gun Mason and Andy would back him up. Charlie was trying to eyeball the silent message to Dave that if he only managed to get off one shot before he was gunned down it would be aimed at him. Charlie saw a momentarily flicker of fear in Dave's eyes. He had got the message and his taut nerves eased somewhat. 'I'm only sayin' what I know,' Dave snarled, and turned away from Charlie and walked across to the stove and helped himself to some coffee.

Mason wasn't keen on gun-play belly to belly close. It cut the odds of a man coming through whole-skinned too low. He reckoned it was time for soft-talking. 'Cool it kid,' he said. 'And you, Dave, back off. We've lost Slim and Bubba, now the two hillbillies; does that look like the shootin' of a played-out old lawman?'

Dave tossed the dregs of his coffee on

to the stove and stormed out of the shack. Whatever mad-assed plan he hoped he could come up with, Charlie thought, to get the better of Mason and his two bully-boys, he would have to think of it real quick. His days with the marauders were numbered. He had faced down Mason twice, he wouldn't get a third go.

Mason came out of the shack with the little dude. They exchanged a few words on the porch that Charlie couldn't make out then the dude got back on to his horse. But he clearly heard the dude's, 'Make it quick, Mason, quick and no fuss'.

Mason turned to Dave. 'Bring Andy in,' he said. 'Then both of you come inside. You, kid, saddle up the horses. The three of you have a job to do in Kansas City.'

EIGHT

Charlie rode with Andy and Dave either side of him, a blank, unconcerned country-boy's look on his face. He was anything but unconcerned inside. He was almost in a state of near panic. Events he had never expected to come up against were rapidly coming to a head. Somehow he would have to try and warn Lars Jackson that his cover had been blown and men had been hired to kill him. Charlie was between a rock and a hard place. He was facing death from two quarters. If he didn't gun down Lars, Dave would get great pleasure in shooting him out of hand. If he made a pretence of going along with the shooting, close enough for Dave to let him draw his gun without Dave being suspicious about his intending to turn it on him and Andy, he would be real close up to Lars. He had seen Lars' hair-trigger reaction to trouble.

He was a man not easily jumped. His first slug would be for the no-good turncoat, Charlie Bannack. And Charlie couldn't blame him. Lars Jackson couldn't read the situation any other way.

The three tied up their horses outside the Plains saloon and walked inside, Charlie still flanked by Dave and Andy. Charlie had made his plan; the only one open to him. He would draw on the two as soon as he saw that he wouldn't endanger any of the saloon's customers. He would get Dave for sure, and die as happy as any man can who doesn't want to die. What happened next depended on his luck. At least the shooting should alert Lars Jackson that something was wrong, though if he was dead the Secret Service man would have to figure out what had gone amiss himself.

If Lady Luck was at his side and he got both of the sons-of-bitches and was still on his feet Charlie hoped that Lars Jackson would have a quiet word with the town marshal to prevent him from stringing him up by the neck for murder. He had a sinking feeling that a dedicated

Secret Service agent like Lars Jackson, wouldn't blow his cover to save the life of some asshole of a drifter, even if he was a temporary President's man. Lars Jackson wouldn't expect or want any other agent to step out of cover for him in the middle of an investigation.

They sat down at an empty table where they had a good view of the bar and Dave buttonholed a barkeep and ordered three whiskies. Charlie cast a searching glance around the bar then asked, 'Is the fella I've got to plug in the place?' He had already seen Lars serving at the far end of the bar, and if it wasn't just a trick of his highly charged nerves, he could have sworn that the wily old fox had him spotted also. He briefly thought of shouting out a warning to Lars but he wouldn't have been able to hear him above the noise of the saloon. Shouting his head off would give Dave and Andy that split-second warning that he had no intention of going through with the scheme and they would all be yanking out guns at the same time. He would lose the slight edge of surprise.

'He's in, kid,' he heard Dave say. 'He's that skull-faced barkeep serving that big bearded fella drinks,' and all his nerves honed in on his right hand slowly sliding down to his pistol. Dave laid a restraining hand on his and Charlie's spirits sank thinking that the marauder had been reading his mind. He had no edge at all now.

'Don't get excited, kid,' Dave said. 'He don't get plugged in here. We wait till the sonuvabitch has finished his shift and goes back to his room. Then we jump him, pick up his gear and his horse so it looks like he's left town for parts unknown.' Dave favoured Charlie with another one of his yellow-fanged fierce smiles. 'Somewhere along the trail where we can bury him deep you'll earn what Mason's payin' you.'

Charlie, playing his role as a genuine, 24–carat Union-hater, drew his hand away from his pistol with a look of disappointment on his face like a kid who had been refused a candy bar. Inside he was a lot more joyous. He had been thrown a lifeline, time. Charlie wracked his brains on how to use that time to warn Lars other than carrying out his original plan of tugging out his gun and taking on Dave and Andy and the more than likely chance of getting himself killed.

He couldn't walk up to the bar on the pretext of buying a round of drinks and pass on the warning to Lars over the bar. That would definitely get him backshot. The sweat popped out of him with all the deep thinking he was putting his brain through. Then Charlie smiled inwardly, then openly as he said, 'You boys won't feel neglected if I take that little redhead standing all by herself at the bar upstairs for a spell. It's a while since I pleasured a woman that purty.'

Dave looked across at the redhead then at Charlie before saying, 'It's OK by us, kid. Don't make a hog of yourself and tire yourself out, you know what's expected of you. When you come down me and Andy will be over at the gaming tables.'

Charlie pushed back his chair and stood up and with a, 'See you boys later', strode towards the girl.

Andy grinned at Dave. 'You're all heart, Dave,' he said.

Dave matched his smile. 'It'll be the last woman, purty or ugly, the kid will get to hump so I hope he enjoys it real good. Keep an eye out for him coming down. Somehow I'm getting a feeling in my guts that the kid ain't who he says he is. If he puts one foot wrong, he's dead.'

In one of the upstairs rooms the redhead introduced herself. 'I'm Rita,' she told Charlie. 'I charge two dollars, mister. Unless you want the special, that's five dollars. Cash before you have your fun.' She sat down on the bed and began pulling her dress over her head.

'Hold it, miss, er, Rita,' Charlie said. 'I ain't brought you up here for that.'

Bare-breasted, dress on her hips, Rita gave Charlie a quizzical look. 'Are you some sort of freak, mister?'

Charlie grinned down at her as he took in the proud, smooth breasts. 'No I sure ain't. It would give me great delight to partake in one of your five-dollar specials but I've got more pressing business to see

128

to. Could get me and another fella killed if it goes wrong. I need your help, and I'm willing to pay the "special treatment" price.'

'Are you the law?' Rita asked. 'Or is the law after you, because I don't want to be dragged into your grief, mister. I've got my own troubles.'

'I'm the law, well sort of,' Charlie replied, experiencing an unusual feeling of chest-expanding pride. 'And you won't get into any trouble, I promise. All I want you to do is to keep the door locked and stay here till I get back.' Charlie smiled encouragingly. 'Now that's a far easier way to earn your five dollars, Rita, ain't it?'

Rita took a long, whore's calculating look at Charlie and, coming up with the opinion that her latest client wasn't a freak or crazy, said, 'OK, mister, I'll do it. The same house rule still applies though, cash in hand.'

'Naturally,' said Charlie. 'Rules are rules.' And he handed Rita a five dollar bill.

Charlie also had Lars puzzled. Lars had

seen him come into the saloon with two pinch-ass-faced characters; he tagged them as owlhooters, and could only think that Mr Bannack had decided to go back to robbing banks. His coming into the saloon was to tell that he had quit working for him and that he could do damn all about it. To go to the law would break his cover and it would soon be all over Kansas City that one of the barkeeps in the Plains saloon was a Secret Service agent. He only hoped that Mr Bannack wouldn't start spreading that news by blabbing to the redhead whore he was taking upstairs.

Charlie entered the saloon by the rear entrance. He had climbed through the window of the redhead's room, on to the balcony and down the back stairs and slipped unseen through the big double doors at the foot of the stairs to find himself in a dimly lit storeroom. He dared not risk going right into the saloon so he waited in the darkness for someone to come in for a barrel of beer or a case of whiskey. Someone who would pass a message on to Mr Jackson. Soon he prayed, before Dave and Andy got restless and suspicious and went upstairs to check things out.

An elderly man carrying a bucket and a mop came into the room and almost dropped his cleaning gear as Charlie stepped out of the shadows.

'It's OK,' Charlie said to the old swamper. 'I ain't here to help myself to your boss's liquor. I'm here to see the tall barkeep. I'd sure be obliged if you would tell him that Charlie Bannack would like a word in his ear, urgent-like.'

The swamper gave Charlie a leery-eyed look then, putting his bucket and mop down, picked up a case of whiskey and headed back into the main bar. Charlie took it that the old man would pass his message on. Just in case it was the bar's owner who came, and armed up, he eased his pistol in its holster. To his relief it was Lars Jackson who showed up, smiling his pleasure at their meeting.

'I'd thought you'd quit on me, Mr Bannack,' he said. 'Gone back to your evil, lawless ways.'

'Ye of little faith,' Charlie replied in a preacher's admonishing voice. Then, voice and features hardening, he began to tell Lars how things had developed. 'I ain't got much time, I'm supposed to be upstairs enjoying the pleasures of a girl, but this Mr M you're tryin' to track down is hereabouts and is wise to....'

'Well I'll be damned!' interrupted a surprised Lars. 'How did you stumble across that gem of information, Mr Bannack?'

'By way of a boss of a gang of marauders and a little fat dude,' answered Charlie. 'But that's neither here nor there at the moment, Mr Jackson. What I've come to tell you is that me and those two hardcases with me have come to town to see you dead. Buried some place where your body will take some finding. Make it look like you've found no joy in Kansas City and moved on out to investigate elsewhere. What do we do now, jump those two before they're wise to us being in cahoots?'

'No, Mr Bannack,' Lars said. 'We go

132

along with the way they've planned it. I take it that they intend grabbing me when I get back to the rooming-house.' Charlie nodded. 'Good,' continued Lars. 'Then we'll surprise them by jumping them there. Any trouble out on the street could involve other people asking awkward questions. Mr M could be nearby ready to lend a hand if things go wrong for his bully boys. Once we've put them where the pair can do us no more harm we'll plan our next move. Does that sound logical to you, Mr Bannack, it's your game as well.'

What sounded logical to Charlie was both of them ass-kicking it out at the State of Kansas real soon, like now. If Mr M failed to kill Lars this time round the unknown bastard would try again and include him in the contract. Charlie's Johnny Reb mad-assed pride triumphed over common, lifesaving sense, as it often had during the war. 'You're the man in charge, Mr Jackson,' he said. 'But don't hold back too long in playing your hand, those two are edgy about me as it is.'

'I won't,' Lars replied. 'You've done a

fine piece of work, Agent Bannack. Now it's time for both of us to get back to where we should be.' Lars grinned. 'Enjoy that redhead for me as well, will you?'

Charlie snorted. 'You must be kiddin', Mr Jackson. Since I came to Kansas I've had to kill four men, wing another and have three men all-fired up to plug me if I so much as fart out of turn. I only hope we'll still be able to talk to each other in the morning this side of Boot Hill.'

Charlie's eyes rounded as he climbed back through the window, Rita lay jaybird naked on the bed. In spite of the queasiness of his stomach he had told Lars about putting him off the desires of the flesh, Charlie's blood began to thicken at his groin. Rita swung her feet on to the floor at the sound of him entering the room and stood up and slipped a robe loosely over her shoulders. Which did nothing to lower the temperature of Charlie's blood.

'Everything OK Rita?' Charlie asked, trying to concentrate his thoughts on the unpleasant things that could happen to him before the night was out. The bad times were certainly coming more frequently and lasting longer than the good times since he became one of the President's men.

'Yeah,' replied Rita. 'Though I thought that I'd better look as though I'm entertaining a client just in case someone came knocking at the door.' Seeing the way Charlie was ogling her Rita slow-smiled. 'Sure you don't want your five dollars worth, mister? I don't mind.'

'I sure know what I would like, Rita,' Charlie mouthed hoarsely. 'But that's not the way its got to be. The men downstairs waiting for me are real mean, impatient men. If I keep them waiting any longer they will come up here and seek me out. Could cause trouble, and you could get hurt.'

An equally disappointed and frustrated Rita moved closer to Charlie and putting her arms around his neck drew him to her and began kissing him. Grinning, she stepped back. 'There,' she said. 'You look as though you've been with a woman. And go down smiling as though you've been having a good time or you'll fool no one. And I'll lose all my clients.'

Charlie switched his mind off thinking about his more pressing thoughts and savoured the feeling of the soft warm lips and body that had been pressing against him, hoping some day that it could be Miss Liz Downes, likewise clad, he would be holding. Charlie took off his coat and, leaving Rita to get her clothes on, walked out of the room. His closing of the door behind him closing the door on his good feelings.

Lars looked at himself in the mirror in the saloon owner's office, the owner being in the bar collecting in the takings. He had discarded his barkeep's apron and was now wearing his hat and coat, ready for the street. Lars flexed his right arm slightly, then came a soft clicking sound and, as suddenly and smoothly as a conjuror's sleight-of-hand trick, an ugly, snub-nosed pistol lay in the palm of his hand. He tried the movement of the spring-action sleeve holster several times before a smile of satisfaction gleamed at him from the mirror.

Lars had seen Charlie coming downstairs, coat over his arm, shirt only part-tucked into his pants, face moon-smiling, and had thought that m'be Charlie had managed to forget his worries long enough for him to enjoy having a woman. On noticing the scowls Charlie was getting from his two companions when he joined them at the gaming tables Lars quickly changed his thinking. A man would have to be blessed with nerves of steel, or not care whether he lived or died, to drop his guard and act normal with those two mean-looking assholes breathing down his neck.

Lars took his time making his way back to his room, stopping to exchange a word with a late-night drinker, one time pausing to light a cigar. Doing nothing that could alarm the two killers following him that would cause them to alter their plans and shoot him down on the street before he and Mr Bannack were ready to take them on. The rooming-house porch when Lars pushed the glass doors open was deserted and he walked along the dimly lit hallway to his room. Behind him his shadowers became solid, hurrying footsteps and, as he opened his door, a pistol was jabbed savagely into the small of his back and he was thrust bodily into his room. Charlie, unexpectedly receiving the same rough treatment.

'What the hell's goin' on,' he protested angrily to Dave. 'Why have you drawn on me? What have I done?'

'Shut your mouth, kid,' Dave said. 'And keep your hands away from your pistol or I'll have to see to the dude myself. You smell wrong, kid, and I aim to keep you on a tight rein. Now give the dude a hand to pack his gear then we can get to hell outa here.'

'I don't know what you expect to find here,' Lars said, playing his part. 'I'm only a barkeep at the Plains saloon. If you sold all you find in this room it wouldn't raise you thirty dollars. Why I'm not even wearing a gunbelt and pistol you could sell, look.' Lars brushed open his jacket.

'We've already been paid, mister,' Dave said. 'So just carry on with your packin' and button up your lip.'

Charlie gave Lars a hurt, you've-dropped-me-right-in-it glance. We jump them in my rooms he had said, Charlie thought, and the long streak didn't even tote a gun. And he had no chance of using his with Dave covering him. To Charlie's surprise Lars gave him a slight nod, a get-ready-for-action nod. How? Was his pardner going to heave the pisspot at them?

Lars fastened his saddle-bags and lifted them up on to his shoulder. As his right hand dropped down it spurted a streak of red, then another. Before the double crack of the pistol died away Dave and Andy were lying on the floor with blood-soaked shirt fronts, Dave breathing his last, Andy already knocking at the gates of hell. And Charlie had only half-drawn his pistol.

'I would have liked to question them,' Lars said, reloading the derringer, eyes still on the men he had shot. 'But they didn't have the cut of talking men and they kinda had me pressed into a corner.'

Charlie let his pistol drop back into its holster. 'I don't know why you took me on, Mr Jackson,' he said. 'You don't need a pardner to watch your back. You're a born loner. What is that little cannon?'

'It's a .45 derringer, a sleeve gun,' Lars said. 'John Wilkes Booth's gun. The one he shot President Lincoln with.' His face formed into the same cold-hardness Charlie had seen on it the first night camp together. 'I hope to use it on this fella M we're trailing if I get close enough to him. Now let's go before anyone comes nosing around wondering what the shooting was all about. By the rear door. It don't do to take any unnecessary chances. Mr M is feeling the pressure of the law closing in on him. With our cover blown we're very vulnerable, Mr Bannack. Anyone who gives us as much as an unkind look will need watching very carefully if we want to stay alive.'

'Mr Jackson,' Charlie said solemnly.

'since I became a President's man I've got used to men tryin' their damnedest to kill me.'

Once clear of Kansas City, with no obvious signs of being trailed, Lars asked Charlie to explain more fully to him just how M knew he was being tracked down.

'I didn't do any findin' out, Mr Jackson,' replied Charlie. 'The information kinda found me.' He then told Lars of the two shoot-outs at the Downes' farm and who he believed was behind them. 'I joined up with Mason's gang of raiders to see if I could scotch their activities. I know that's not what you sent me out for, Mr Jackson, but being a sodbuster myself it got my blood up to see honest, hard-workin' folk being forced off their land. While I was with Mason at his hole-up he got a visit from a little dude. The next thing was that me and those two boys you saw off were riding to Kansas City to see you likewise.'

Lars smiled inwardly. Mr Bannack was an uncomplicated man to read. He had no doubts that the young Miss Liz Downes, whom Mr Bannack had hardly mentioned, had a lot to do with his decision to join up with the marauders. 'That's m'be so, Mr Bannack,' he said. 'but coincidental or not you came by the information and that's all that counts in our profession. One thing is for sure if you hadn't been with the gang I wouldn't be alive now. Regarding your theory about Mr Lindford as the man behind the land-grabbing, did you pick up any solid evidence supporting your suspicions from any of the gang? Mr Lindford rides tall in Kansas. Well thought of in Washington. The law would need cast-iron proof before they would dare haul him up in front of a judge and jury.'

'No I ain't got any evidence, Mr Jackson,' Charlie said. 'But I know it in here.' Charlie tapped his chest. 'The same way Dave knew I wasn't a Union hater. I just know that's all.'

Lars let that line of questioning drop. 'Getting back to M,' he said, 'did you find out anything about his messenger, the little dude?'

'No,' said Charlie. 'I tried to pump Dave for his name but he kept his lips buttoned up. How Mr M knew you were working in Kansas City as a barkeep is something else I don't know.' Charlie grinned. 'I ain't a real Secret Service man, Mr Jackson.'

'We'll just have to pay your old boss a visit then, Mr Bannack,' Lars said. 'Mason seems the man anyone who wants some dirty work doing hires. He might be more forthcoming regarding the dude.' Lars didn't doubt or accept Charlie's considered opinion of Lindford being a land-grabber. By profession and training he took in everything he heard, dismissing nothing as fanciful or downright lies till carefully assessed. He was well aware that the big men in industry and commerce cut corners in the building of their financial empires. Lindford would only be following a trend. And the way he earned his money wasn't Secret Service business however much he would have liked to help out Mr Bannack's friends, the Downes.

Lars jerked up in his saddle, face

tightening with barely controlled excitement, as he yanked his horse to a sudden halt. Charlie pulled up alongside him, grabbing for his rifle. 'Anything the matter, Mr Jackson, can you smell trouble coming our way?'

'No,' replied Lars, gazing vacant-eyed ahead of him. 'It's just that I've got the same feeling inside me about Mr Lindford as you have, Mr Bannack, he's more twisted than you thought. Lindford and the man who wrote that letter to Booth are the same person. The land-grabbing sonuvabitch is our Mr M!'

'How do you come to that reckonin'?' asked a surprised Charlie.

Lars brought his gaze back on Charlie. 'If we accept that Lindford is eyeballs deep into land-grabbing now, paying men like Mason to drive farmers off their holdings it doesn't take much more reasoning that Mason, or some other brush-boy chief, was doing the same for him during the war. How else would a dude businessman like Lindford know, or know of men who had contact with Missouri raiders,

Mr Bannack? You don't hire scum like them by putting a wanted ad in the local newssheet. No, the more I chew on it the surer I am that Lindford is a Copperhead, and the fella we're after.' Lars struck his fist angrily against his thigh. 'But proving it isn't going to be easy, Mr Bannack. If we can't nail him for land-grabbing what chance have we to prove to a court that he was a traitor to the Union.'

'We'll just have to lean on Mason real hard, Mr Jackson,' Charlie said. He grinned. 'I'm looking forward to seeing his ugly-mug when I tell him he's lost the last of his boys.'

'Let's go then, Mr Bannack,' Lars said, 'and pass on that joyous news to him.' And both of them kneed their horses into a trail-eating trot.

NINE

Thomas M. Lindford felt the acidity of bile clawing at the back of his throat. He had heard about the shootings through one of his regular, get-together, brandy-and-cigar meetings with his fellow businessmen of Kansas City. And the disappearance of a newly hired barkeep of the Plains saloon in whose room the dead men had been found.

There was the occasional wounding, knife and pistol inflicted, fist fights, between men whose blood was inflamed by the amount of strong liquor they had downed, over pleasuring the same woman or losses at cards. If it came to killing it was done out in Main Street or in the saloons, publicly. The killings in the room were different, cold and deliberate. The men had gone into the room to kill, not to call someone out. Grudge killings,

146

the experts opined. The settling of old scores between Missouri brush boys and Col Lane's 'Red Legs'. Who was who baffled the same experts.

It was no mystery to Lindford. Mason's men had made a balls-up of what they had been paid to do. His balls. He tried to convince himself that things were exactly as they had been. The Secret Service man could not link him with Booth. But as another wave of sickness came shooting up from his stomach he knew that they were not. The son-of-a-bitch might not know who he was looking for but he would know that he was getting close to him, scaring him into making a move. The hangman's noose swung ominously in front of Lindford's mind's eye.

Lindford contemplated sending Freedman to Mason again. Get the marauder to hunt the barkeep down, no expense spared. The bastard wouldn't be too far away knowing that he was trailing a hot lead. Then again, thought Lindford, Freedman or Mason might make a panicky move and draw attention to him. The safest thing he could do was to sit it out. Wait till the Secret Service man showed himself again or was dragged in by the law for questioning about the killings. The need for Mason would come then. That reasoning settled Lindford's queasy stomach, though when he lit up his eight-inch Havana it still smoked like horse droppings.

Augustus Freedman was also having thoughts on the shooting. He wasn't aware of Lindford's connection with Booth. He had first tagged the barkeep as an undercover Pinkerton investigating the raids on the farms along the border and had possibly come too close to unmasking the man behind the raids, Mr Lindford. Somehow that explanation didn't settle easy on Freedman's mind.

Then, thinking like a former spy, Freedman began to conjure up all the possibilities of who the killing target was and why he was in Kansas City. And more important, why had Lindford been that shit-scared at him showing up that he wanted him dead. His first opinion that the man was a Pinkerton didn't hold water. He had noticed no extra toing-and-froing at the Pinkerton office since the shooting. No worried look on the agency chief's face at the sudden disappearance of one of his operators.

The barkeep certainly wasn't a State Marshal. They did their snooping around with badges on their shirts; and they would have had the backing of local law enforcement officers in any action they took. And a marshal would have not gone to ground after the shooting. That only left, however far-fetched it seemed, concluded Freedman, only one probability, the barkeep was a Secret Service agent. He didn't have to raise any sweat pondering on what the agent's mission in Kansas City was. The Secret Service only worked on cases that involved the security of the State and threats against the President or heads of government departments. One president had been assassinated and the search for all who were party to the killing was still going on. The big hunt had reached as far as Kansas City. Mr

Thomas M. Lindford being the quarry, Freedman thought confidently. Somehow Lindford was tied in with the killing of Abe Lincoln, Freedman cursed. Now he was also by-passing Lindford's orders to Mason to get rid of the agent.

He was in deep trouble. Being implicated in a failed plot to murder a Secret Service agent wasn't a hanging offence. But the Secret Service swung a wide net and they would soon discover that he had been a reb spy. No amount of protesting his innocence about having had any dealings with Booth and any other of the plotters, swearing on Bibles or his grey-haired mother's grave, would stay his fate. Once a dirty reb spy, always a dirty reb spy. Still working to bring down the Union government by any dirty way he could. From then on in it would be a non-stop gallop to the gallows in Washington.

Freedman began to take stock of his situation more calmly. He hadn't been caught yet and one thing was for certain, he would be damned if he was just going to sit on his ass and do nothing to prevent it happening. Of the men who could finger him as the man who had brought the orders to kill the barkeep-cum-Secret Service agent only two were still alive. Mason, and the kid he had seen on Mason's stoop. Mason could more than describe his looks to any interested parties, he knew his haunts, could tell them where he could be found. Mason had outlived his usefulness. Freedman cold-smiled. Sentimentality and business didn't mix. Especially not in the important business of keeping Augustus Freedman alive.

The kid, not lying dead with Dave and Andy, puzzled Freedman. The Secret Service agent could have taken him alive for questioning, or, he thought briefly, the kid was also a government agent. Though he couldn't picture an ex-reb turning completely over this close to the end of the war to work for the Union against his own kind. Unless he had been working under cover all along. Whoever he was he had to accept that the kid would have told the Union agent all he knew about him, and that for his peace of mind wasn't much. They had only seen each other once. Mason was the real threat. Once Mason was eliminated then it would be getting-out-of-Kansas-fast time. Eastwards, to St Louis, m'be as far as Chicago, where they would never find him. Another fact he had to accept was that the Union agent would be riding fast to the next link in the chain leading to the man he was trying to hunt down, Mason. He had to beat him to the marauder leader.

TEN

Mason had had a bad night, the pain from his wound not easing up at all. If it was still as sore when Dave and Andy and the kid came back from Kansas City he would send one of them to Little Creek to bring the doc out to the shack to fix his shoulder. As soon as it had healed up enough for him to ride he and the boys would pay another visit to the Downes place to wind up some unfinished business. Mason's face twisted in a bared-toothed angry grimace. This time more sneaky-like so that he could gut-shoot the son-of-a-bitch rifleman if he was still hanging around. The snarl changed into a no less fierce apology of a grin. Then he would use the girl real good.

Painfully he eased himself out of his cot and struggled, one-handed, to pull on his boots, before going outside to relieve himself and almost bumped into the kid standing on the porch. Mason, rubbing the sleep from his eyes asked where Dave and Andy were. With his vision cleared he got a stomach-churning feeling that he had wasted his breath asking the question. The kid's grin and the rifle inches from his chest explained it all. Dave and Andy were, along with the rest of the boys, dead.

Mason did some under-the-breath cursing. Dave had been right about the kid. He should have plugged the double-timing bastard when he had first stood up to him. Shown the kid who was running the outfit. Slit-eyed with concentration, Mason faced Charlie. It wasn't the first tight spot he had been in and although the kid had the edge now he was a long way from being cornered.

Mason heard movement along the porch to the left of him and a tall, Indian-faced man, also holding a rifle on him, stepped into view. Mason's hopes sank. He knew a professional manhunter when he saw one. He also had the uneasy feeling that he was eyeballing the man Dave and Andy had been sent to kill. Catching him off-guard wasn't going to be easy.

'I guess you've cottoned on to the fact that Dave and Andy won't be ridin' in, Mason,' Charlie said.

Mason killed him dead with a venomous glare.

'We want to know about the dude who brings you the messages from someone, as yet unknown, in Kansas City,' Lars said. 'Names, places and suchlike.'

Mason favoured Lars with the same drop-dead look he had given Charlie.

Lars retaliated by giving Mason's wound a not too gentle tap with his rifle barrel that brought a howl of pain from Mason and a sympathetic wince from Charlie.

'You bastard!' Mason cried, eyes blinded by tears. 'You lowdown stinkin' bastard!'

'I'm an impatient man, Mr Mason,' Lars growled. 'So I would advise you to answer my question. You may not know it but you've got yourself mixed up in serious trouble. To spell it out for you, with a man who was involved in the plot to kill President Lincoln.'

155

With the pain he was still feeling it took Mason a few seconds to take in what he was being accused of. 'I had nothin' to do with Lincoln's killin',' he screeched, in a voice as high-pitched as an hysterical girl's. 'Why I ain't been more than thirty miles from where I'm standin' right now since before the war. You can nail me for raidin' the Kansas farmers but you ain't railroadin' me on that charge!'

'That's m'be so, Mr Mason,' Lars said. 'But you did send your boys on that man's instructions to kill me, a Government agent investigating Lincoln's murder. That's implication after the fact. Enough to see you dancing on air at the end of a rope. They're in a real hanging mood back in Washington. So, tell me the name of the man who brought the orders and m'be I'll be able to clear it for you so that you'll only do time for your raiding activities.'

Mason's frightened bluster went from his face. Charlie thought that the marauder was going to pass out as Lars raised his rifle in a threatening gesture again. Mr

Lars was a real mean gent when roused, though he conceded that the war had never ended for the Secret Service. And wars, as he well knew, weren't fought with soft gloves. If it had been Mason who was asking the questions he wouldn't have wasted his time with 'please', and 'if you don't mind, thank you', sweet-talk crap.

Freedman drew up his horse sharply on the edge of the clearing. He had seen Mason standing on the porch with, he thought naturally, two of his boys till a second look showed that they were holding rifles on Mason. One of the men he recognized as the newest member of Mason's gang. The tall man could only be the Union Secret Service agent. The sons-of-bitches had been quick off the mark. Freedman smiled. The luck was running his way now. The three men who were a threat to his wellbeing were all in one place, within rifle range. He quickly dismounted and led his horse deeper into the timber. Then pulling out his rifle walked back to the clearing again.

'All right! All right!' Mason said. 'I'll

tell you what I know, but it ain't much.' Nervously he eyed Lars' raised rifle. 'On one condition, you don't try and pin any takin' part in the shootin' down of Abe Lincoln. Is it a deal?'

'I think that could be arranged,' Lars said. 'If what you're going to tell me is real helpful. We'll start off with the name of the man I asked you for; who is the little dude?'

'Gus Freedman,' replied Mason instantly. Feeling a little more confident that he could escape a hanging he tried a weak smile. 'Freedman used to work behind your blue-belly lines during the war. I meet up with him once a month or so in Macey's bar in Lawrence, across the border in Kansas, to get my due or any fresh orders. If he ain't there he'll leave a letter for me behind the bar. Who he works for I don't know. All I know is he works for someone who wants you dead.' Mason's smile almost reached his eyes. 'In fact Freedman said the killin' of you was urgent. It musta been, Freedman ain't a regular visitor to this shack. And that's all

158

I can tell you, mister. I couldn't tell you any more even if I was standing over the drop with a rope round my neck pleadin' for mercy.' His smile was replaced by a worried-eyed look as he waited to see if the big man thought that he had given him enough helpful information to prevent him from dancing on air.

Lars reckoned that Mason had told him all he knew. Facing a possible hanging a man tends to become loose-mouthed. If Lars had wanted to question Mason any further he wouldn't have got the chance. The red spouting hole that suddenly appeared in Mason's forehead and the sound of the shot that put it there came almost simultaneously. Lars spun round at the sound of the shot and the shell that should have struck him in the back, tearing into his heart, caught him on the side, slicing deep across his ribs to glance upwards and though his lower right arm. Lars gasped with pain and dropped to his knees, his rifle falling from his hands, then keeled over completely to lie in a crumpled heap on his side.

The few seconds between Mason falling back against the wall of the shack and sliding to the boards dead, and the third shot aimed at him, was enough time for Charlie's highly war-trained survival nerves to react. He flung himself down below the porch floor as the shot chipped slivers off the porch post he had been standing beside, and took a veteran's stock of his situation.

There was only one sniper firing from the left of the trail that led into the clearing. Looking along the porch he could hear by Lars' groaning he hadn't ended up like Mason, yet. If Lars made any movement the sniper would target him again, aiming more accurately, a killing shot. That thought decided Charlie's only course of action. He leapt to his feet and ran, low and zigzagging, towards the sniper's position, yelling the rebel yell and pumping off Spencer loads. The mad-assed charge at Cemetery Ridge all over again. On a smaller scale but nonetheless still highly dangerous for him.

The barrage of shells whistled too close

for comfort around Freedman, one nicking his ear drawing blood and, like Charlie had, Freedman made a quick decision. To get the hell out of it. If he hadn't stopped the hunt permanently by not shooting down dead the son-of-a-bitch fireballing in on him he had delayed it, given him time to put his affairs right in Kansas City and catch a Kansas-Pacific eastbound to Chicago. He turned and ran back to his horse.

Charlie, his rifle empty, had reached the trees and, slowing to a prowling walk, drew his pistol to close in on the sniper. He heard the sound of a fast-moving horse and straightened up, stopping his cautious-footed progress, breathing like a winded horse, pistol hand shaking. 'Charlie,' he said. 'it's a good job that fella took off. The way you're tremblin' you couldn't have hit a horse from three feet away. You're too nervy for this Secret Service lark.'

He waited, listening, just in case the man who had been doing the shooting was about to come ass-kicking it out of the timber behind him to catch him unawares. Satisfied that the small battle was definitely over Charlie ran back to see to Lars. Lars was still conscious, only just, but was losing a lot of blood. Charlie stepped over Mason's dead body to go inside the shack, a quick look round and he saw some shirts lying in a heap on a chair. They weren't too clean but they would have to do; Lars couldn't go on losing blood.

The nearest doctor, Charlie reckoned, would be in Little Creek, so could the man who had shot Lars. Palmers Flats would be the safest place. It was a longer ride but there he could ask Liz's pa to look out for Lars while he rode on to Lawrence to have it out with Gus Freedman. It didn't take a trained Secret Service agent to figure out that Freedman could be the only candidate who could be listed as the shootist.

Lars became fully conscious while Charlie was levering him up into a sitting position with his back against the front of the shack so that he could strap up his wounds. 'You OK, Mr Bannack,' he weakly asked.

'Yeah, I'm fine,' replied Charlie. 'But

you ain't so good. They seem clean wounds but you'll need a doc. Once I bandage you up we can go and find one. Mason ain't so lucky, he's dead.'

'What about the fella who was doing the shooting?' Lars said. 'I opine that it could only be the Mr Freedman Mason told us about.'

'Me too,' Charlie said. 'The sonuvabitch is long gone.' He grinned. 'He didn't like the sound of the rebel yell.'

'I never thought that that caterwauling would have scared off a Southerner,' Lars said. He gave Charlie a faint, lopsided grin. 'When you left me at Kansas City I expected to hear of you being shot at by some ex-blue belly, not by a fellow reb.'

Charlie managed to get Lars up on to his saddle without causing him too much pain, if he had the stone-faced blue belly wasn't showing it. 'OK, Mr Jackson,' Charlie said. 'Grit your teeth, I'm taking you to see some friends of mine.' He drew the Spencer out of its boot, checked its action and rested it across his knees, then heeled his horse into a walk, holding on to Lars' reins, thinking that if Freedman was waiting somewhere along the trail to finish off what he had started at the shack it would be like Gettysburg again, and coming through three Gettysburgs all in one piece was asking for a hell of a lot of luck.

Behind them smoke and gouts of flame belched out of the door and windows of the shack as the fire took hold. Charlie hadn't the time to see to it that Mason had been decently covered up, Lars came first. Yet he didn't think it was Christian-like to leave even a murdering asshole like Mason where wolves and coyotes and suchlike scavengers could chew at his body so he had dragged the corpse into the shack and put it to the torch. Charlie had read somewhere that in some foreign countries it was a regular way of getting rid of the dead. If he had read it wrong Mason was in no position to come back at him. Attending to the living always came first; if the one alive was your buddy, more so.

ELEVEN

Liz Downes, coming out of Logan's dry-goods store, Palmers Flats, saw Mr Bannack riding past leading a horse with its rider half-bowed in his saddle. She gasped in alarm, almost dropping her packages, as she ran across to him, praying frantically that Mr Bannack hadn't also been hurt.

Charlie saw her and drew both horses to a halt. The tension of riding shotgun over Mr Jackson, as well as watching out for his own hide, eased on seeing her. Smiling broadly he touched his hat in greeting as she stood alongside his mount looking up at him. A worried, concerned look, which made Charlie feel as though he was really riding tall.

'Are you....you're not hurt, Mr Bannack, are you?' Liz said. Certain that she must be in love with him otherwise how could she get so flustered speaking to him, and burning as if stricken by swamp-water fever. And if he had been lying across his saddle like his companion she didn't know how she would have reacted. Swooned, she had no doubts.

'No I'm OK, Miss Liz,' Charlie replied, still full-faced smiling. 'But I've got to find a doctor for my friend, Mr Jackson, here, he's been gunshot.'

More confusing for Liz was that she felt the tears running down her cheeks when she was feeling so happy. Mr Bannack would be thinking that she was just a scatterbrained young girl, not capable of helping to run a farm if Mr Bannack, feeling the same way towards her as she did to him, asked her pa for her hand in marriage. Blinking back her tears she said, 'Doctor Lister's surgery is just across the street, next to the saloon, Mr Bannack. But I think that he's in the saloon playing poker with my pa.' She smiled at Lars. 'I'll go and seek him out for you, Mr Jackson.'

Lars watched her skirt scuff the dust as she ran over to the saloon. In spite of the pain and discomfort he was feeling he managed a smile.

'Fine sensible gal you've got yourself, Mr Bannack,' he said. Thinking that if he had been as young as the kid he would have taken time off tracking down Mr M and helped her and her pa out.

'Ah heck, Mr Jackson,' Charlie said, colouring up. 'I ain't got her at all. What can she see in me, a broke-to-the-wide ex-reb? And another thing, what happened back there at the shack, and the shootin's before, don't encourage me to raise any hopes concerning my future expectations. I could die a broke-to-the-wide ex-reb.' Charlie tugged at Lars' horse's reins. 'Let's go and see that sawbones before Mr Freedman gets too big a lead on us.'

'You do as the doc says, Mr Jackson,' Charlie said. 'Lie up for a week or so.'

Doc Lister, a small-framed man, smelling of whiskey fumes and cigar smoke, seemed to Charlie, no stranger himself to seeing men having their wounds treated, to have made a good job of cleaning up Mr Jackson's injuries. When he had finished the strapping of bandages tightly across Lars' chest Doc Lister straightened up and professionally-eyed his patient.

'It ain't my business to ask you how you came by these wounds,' he said, 'but if you had to go and get yourself shot you couldn't have got nicer, cleaner looking wounds. Though it's going to hurt like hell for a spell till those cracked ribs knit together. So you can put off getting back on to your horse till they do so or they could puncture your lungs and you'll need the undertaker not a doctor.'

'You can rest up at Uncle Phil's place; he has a spare room,' Liz said. 'Can't he, Pa?'

Mr Downes, who had come from the saloon with Doc Lister, agreed with his daughter's suggestion. 'No problem at all, Mr Jackson,' he said. 'Me and Liz are beholden to Mr Bannack, so any friend of his is a friend of me and my kin.'

Charlie could see the refusal of Mr Downes' offer in Lars' eyes. Him being the breed of man who would be near knocking on the Pearly Gates before he would call it a day and rest-up.

'You take up Mr Downes' offer, Mr Jackson,' he said. 'Ain't no sense in ridin' around and opening up that wound.' Trying to keep a straight face he eyed Lars like a Dutch uncle. 'And I sure don't want to rely on a lame duck backing me up if I get into a tight corner.'

Lars jerked angrily up from the chair. 'Why you young....' he gasped, then fell back with a loud groan of pain. The doc was right, he thought. The girl was right and Mr Bannack doubly so. So far the tracking down of M had been rough, a tally of seven dead men by his and Mr Bannack's hands, and it could get a good deal rougher before it ended. His natural disappointment, feeling that he was getting close to unmasking M, and m'be wouldn't be there at the final showdown, was clouding his professional judgement. And that was dangerous. He had no right to expect Mr Bannack to risk his life more than he had been doing since they had left Washington. Riding with him in the unhelpful state he was in went above and well beyond the call of duty for a man whom he had arm-twisted into becoming a President's man. Lars also noticed the favouring looks Miss Downes was casting at Mr Bannack. He wouldn't like to face her if he got her beau killed, needlessly or otherwise.

Lars, with some effort, and a great deal of pain, levered himself up from the couch again. 'I'll do as you all say,' he growled. He smiled at Liz. 'How could I turn down the offer of being attended to by such a pretty nurse.'

Although a blushing Miss Downes gave him a sweet-smiling look for his compliment Lars guessed that she would far rather been tending to the kid's every want than fetching and carrying for an old fart like him.

Liz and her pa had left Charlie to bring Lars along to her uncle's place at his own speed while they went on ahead to prepare the room for the unexpected guest at the farm. Once there Lars made a firm stand against being put to bed by saying that he would be as comfortable resting up in the rocking-chair on the front porch, if that was OK with Caleb Downes' brother. Having to go to bed when it was time for sleeping was soon enough. The hard-nosed stance was all blow-hard show. Lars felt like crawling into bed and slowly passing away.

Charlie, after seeing to the horses, had eaten a meal specially prepared for him by Liz and was now ready to saddle-up and ride out and pick up Freedman's trail. Like Lars he wasn't showing his real feelings. He would have much rather stayed on at the farm mooning over Miss Liz, but he had given his word to Lars, and to himself, to help Liz and her pa hold on to their land. If he had reasoned correctly both missions were linked together, by Mr Lindford.

Lars was sitting on the porch talking to Caleb Downes when Charlie joined them to tell Lars that he was about to ride out. Earlier on he tried to say his goodbyes to Miss Downes while she was working in the kitchen but as soon as she saw him enter she had grabbed a bowl of feed from the table and ran out of the kitchen to the henhouse, dashing a surprised Charlie's hopes more than somewhat of a closer, friendlier relationship with her, making him think that a man never knew how he stood with a woman, especially one he wishfully hoped had a leaning towards him.

'Take no chances with Freedman if you catch up with him, Mr Bannack,' Lars said. 'I should like to question him about Lindford, see if he can be persuaded to point the finger at Lindford, prove us right, to save his own neck. But if you have to, you shoot the son-of-a-bitch, understand?'

Charlie nodded. What Lars had said was how he was going to play it if Freedman cut up rough. His mad-assed days were over, and the reason they were gone was busy feeding the hens.

'I don't know who you gents are trailin',' Caleb Downes said. 'You could be a pair of owlhoots, Pinkertons, bounty hunters, whatever, it don't matter to me. But if you don't think that I'm poking my nose into something that don't concern me I'd like to give Mr Bannack a piece of advice.'

'Mr Downes,' Charlie said, 'a man would be a durn fool if he didn't listen to advice honestly given; say what's on your mind.'

'I heard Mr Jackson mention the township of Lawrence,' Caleb Downes said. 'If you're intendin' goin' there I wouldn't go ridin' in wearing that Johnny Reb coat. Lawrence has had a visit from you rebs, twice. They left an unpleasant taste in the citizens' mouths. Catch some of them in a bad mood, war officially over or not, they'll take a great pleasure in stringin' you up, Mr Bannack.'

'I reckon that's sound advice, Mr Downes,' Charlie said. 'I ain't seeking extra trouble. I'll take it off and pack it in my saddle-bag before I go.'

'Are you still all ears, Mr Bannack?' Caleb continued. 'Because I ain't finished dishin' out the advice.'

'As I said, Mr Downes,' Charlie replied. 'I ain't too proud to listen to anything that will make my trip easier.'

'Then go and see my daughter before you ride out,' Caleb said. 'She's bawlin' her head off in the henhouse. If you don't settle her down somehow she'll lead me a helluva dance that's for sure.'

A poker-faced Lars looked at Charlie. 'Do as Mr Downes says, Mr Bannack, Freedman can gain a few more minutes on us. I don't want an uptight female tending to me. One who will already be bearing a grudge against me for sending you away on a dangerous mission.'

Freedman looped left once he had crossed over into Kansas, to make a call at Lawrence to see to it that his back-trail was covered. The way Mason had fallen Freedman reckoned that he was good and dead. Though that didn't mean the marauder hadn't blabbed all that he knew about him before he was silenced forever. Trained as a spy he had to dismiss hopes and m'be's from his calculating the outcome of any situation he found himself up against. He dealt in facts or highly conceivable facts. One such

174

probability that the kid working with the Union agent knew of his and Mason's meeting place in Lawrence. Having not been fortunate enough to have downed the kid probability number two was that sometime, not too far ahead, the kid, or another agent, would show up in Lawrence to pick up his trail.

The ending, permanently of that threat presented no problem to Freedman. There were men in Lawrence who would see to it, if well paid, that the only way any Union-snooper would leave Lawrence would be feet first, on his way to Boot Hill.

As he neared Lawrence, Charlie put from his mind the pleasant, bittersweet few minutes he'd had with Liz before leaving the farm. The kisses and the tears as she clung to him, pleading with him to take care of himself. He opined it was time to put that promise into practice. He drew up his mount and checked that the Colt and the Spencer were in good working order and loaded for bear. He had declined Lars' offer of his sleeve gun on the grounds that if he ever had to use it there would be more than a good chance of him blowing off his own fingers.

Charlie didn't expect to come face to face with Freedman in Lawrence, reckoning that he would be holed-up someplace further west in Kansas. That reasoning didn't allow Charlie to breathe more easily, or to be ready to jump and shoot in any direction, when he rode into town. Freedman had been callous enough to kill Mason, a man hired by him, to protect himself and the man behind him. He couldn't see Freedman leaving himself wide open now. Other hard-assed assholes like Mason and his boys could be lying in wait for him. Charlie heeled his horse into a walk, skin tightening across his cheekbones. If any son-of-a-bitch gave him as much as a leery-eyed look he would plug him. Miss Liz Downes wouldn't expect anything less from him.

Charlie strode into Macey's bar on the balls of his feet. Nerves screwed up taut as they had been the last few seconds before the slow, purposeful march towards a

Union line broke into a wild, yelling mad-assed charge. He went up to the bar and ordered a drink from a loose-jowled, slack-bellied barkeep. The eyes that watched him down his whisky were out of keeping with the barkeep's flabby-gutted physique. They were hard and unblinking like a rattler contemplating its next victim.

'Mason sent me here to see Mr Freedman,' Charlie said, confident-voiced. 'He's busted an arm, won't be able to get astride his horse for a spell.' Charlie's smile was as confident as his voice. 'Is he around?'

Charlie noticed a slight twitching of the barkeep's hound-dog jowls and his eyes flickered nervously away from him to the two men standing further along the bar to his right. If Charlie hadn't got the message that he had walked headlong into a setup the barkeep's loud-voiced answer of, 'No, mister, Mr Freedman ain't been in. Don't know when he's due in', rang the alarm bells in his head.

Charlie's nerves tightened up another notch. Managing to fake a disappointed look he said, 'I'll just have to hang around in town a spell and call in later to see if he's showed up. Tell him it's Bannack, one of Mason's men who wants to see him if he comes up to the bar. He'll know who you mean.'

'I'll do that, Mr Bannack,' replied the barkeep, lying as easily as Charlie. And again he was finding it difficult to hold his eyes on Charlie.

Charlie took his time with his drink as he weighed-up what he had to face gazing in the flyblown bar mirror. The fact that the lard-bellied barkeep hadn't cast his snake-eyed look in any other direction seemed to indicate to Charlie that there were only two men to take on. He didn't allow his thoughts to dwell too long on there being more of Freedman's hired bully-boys outside on the street waiting for the word to jump on him. There was no sense in adding to his already known worries.

Charlie believed that he had a slight edge over the opposition, stronger than just a belief, because he was risking his life on that advantage. Firstly, he knew where the threat was coming from and secondly he wore no pistol belted about his belly, he was shirt-carrying the Colt.

The two gunmen would be pissing their pants with laughter at the thought of how easy it was going to be to earn Freedman's money, putting paid to a man who wasn't armed up. Fooling them into making their play slow and foolishly fatal for them, or so Charlie opined. Charlie was realizing that he was banking on more hopes than a repenting sinner praying for salvation on his deathbed. His last hope before finishing his drink and making a move to bring things to a head was that he wasn't about to be laid out on his deathbed.

Charlie's plan was no great shakes. He hadn't the time to work out any grand stratagem. He intended to turn his back on the two as he left the bar. Reckoning that to a couple of dry-gulchers it would be too much of an invite for them not to start pulling out their guns to cut him down. Although it was a high-risk play, beating two men to the draw, Charlie

179

wasn't being entirely foolhardy. He would keep a wary-eyed, sidelong glance in the bar mirror for any sign of movement from the gunmen and, as soon as his back was to them, he would have his gun out of his shirt and held, fully cocked, across his chest.

Whatever happened it would have to appear to the rest of the bar's customers that he was the innocent party in the shoot-out. Otherwise he would waste a lot of valuable time explaining to the law how it came about that he pulled a gun on two men whom he had never met before, minding their own business standing drinking peacefully at the bar. And not getting a word of it believed. Before Mr Jackson could be contacted to back up his statement he could be swinging by the neck on the hanging tree for the crime of double murder. A trial and its outcome didn't take long in a frontier town.

Charlie patted the Colt lying heavy but comfortingly against his skin. Making sure that it could be yanked out without hindrance. He emptied his glass and braced himself for the next few hectic, nerve-racking seconds, time at the end of which, he thought sourly, he could be dead, or as near to it that didn't matter. Movement in the bar mirror caught his eye and stayed his hand. The two men, drinks in their hands, were coming along the bar towards him. The sons-of-bitches had made a plan of their own.

Charlie poured himself another drink, trying hard to appear normal and unconcerned. The gunmen positioned themselves on either side of him and Charlie, elbows resting on the bar, gave them both a lone drinker's noncommittal cursory glance. This close up he could see how the pair earned their keep in their hard, dead-eyed, unshaven faces. The man on Charlie's left, a small, weedy-framed man, made up for his stunted growth by wearing a heavy calibre Colt sheathed in a well-filled shell belt, cross-drawn fashion, that dragged at the top of his pants. The other man, more Charlie's build, favoured a pistol on either hip. Fancying himself as a real shootist,

Charlie fleetingly thought. The blood began to seeth and pop in Charlie's ears as loud as pistol discharges as he watched and waited, dead-panfaced, in the mirror for them to make their play.

The little man opened up the game. Charlie saw him pick up his glass and pour his drink over the bar top then he stepped back a pace and glared up at him.

'Did you see that, Marvin?' the little man cried. 'The clumsy son-of-a-bitch spilt my drink. I reckon he owes me an apology, and another whisky!'

Charlie knew the play. The little bastard would hold his attention while his buddy did the shooting. A knife or a pistol would be placed in his hand as he fell to the floor and it would be their words against a dead man's that they were only defending themselves. Sure enough Charlie saw the big man's hand sneak down to the butt of one of his pistols. Charlie straightened up from the bar, right hand reaching inside his shirt. He cut loose at the big man with his pistol still under his shirt, the powder flash searing painfully across his bare chest.

The gunman took the shell in his right shoulder, tearing into flesh and muscles, shattering bones. The shock to his nervous system so severe that it blacked him out before his voice could register the fearful pain of the wound and he dropped heavily to the floor like a man already dead. Charlie's gun was out in the open. In a savage downward swing he laid it hard against the little man's head and felled him to floor as soundless about his pain as his compadre, his big gun still undrawn.

Charlie swung away from the bar, eyes wide and wild, set in a strained, white face. 'You all saw what happened!' he almost shouted. 'I was having a quiet drink on my own and those two ganged up on me. Men I've never seen before. They must have been drunk or loco!'

'We saw, mister,' a man said, sitting at a nearby table. 'Those two sonsuvbitches went out of their way to get at you. Slattery, get that *hombre* with the busted shoulder to the doc before all the blood he's spilling spoils your nice, clean sawdust.'

Charlie turned and fierce-eyed the fat

183

barkeep, pistol still fisted, and pointing in his direction. 'Has Freedman paid any more assholes to gun me down? And where is the little dude now? I want answers, no crap, or by hell they'll be three men lying in here for the doc to treat.'

Slattery's face grew slacker with fear. He hadn't seen men downed so quick and by a sneaky trick of shirt-carrying a pistol. The same cannon the Indian-faced kid was aiming at his guts. 'They're the only two I had to tell if anyone showed up asking for Freedman,' his voice a fear-dried croak. 'Freedman ain't in town, he left just after he told me what to do. And that's all I know, mister, honest.' He gazed at Charlie with the fixed, hypnotic stare of a jack-rabbit being eyeballed by a rattler.

Charlie fish-eyed him for a few more minutes then said, 'OK I believe you. You can see to your late drinkers' needs and explain to the local lawman that their wrongdoing got them the way they are.' He pushed the Colt back into his shirt, wincing as the hammer brushed against the angry, raised, red-weal of the powder-burn, and left the bar.

As Charlie was unhitching his horse he was joined by the man who had spoken up for him inside the bar.

'I heard you askin' that fat slob, Slattery, where Freedman was,' he said. 'M'be I can help you, that's if you don't think I'm being too nosy.'

Charlie smiled. 'You ain't, mister, keep talkin'.'

'I used to work for Queenie Stewart,' the man continued. 'Owner of the classiest whorehouse in Kansas City. Her girls were for the delights of the bigshots of the town, the mayor, the top army brass from the military post and Mr Big himself, Thomas Magnus Lindford. What should interest you, mister, was that Mr Freedman was also a regular visitor to Queenie's. If he ain't in Kansas City now, m'be Queenie, or one of her girls could point you in the same direction he took off in.'

'Well I'll be damned,' breathed Charlie. 'Thomas *Magnus,* the M who signed the letter to Booth.' The link between

Freedman and him had been established. His and Mr Jackson's reasoning had been right. Lindford was a Copperhead. He thanked the man for his information and told him he would check it out.

'Ain't no need to thank me, mister,' the man replied. 'In my book if a man has a difference of opinion with another fella he should settle it face to face. Not hire bully-boys to do his fightin' for him.'

On the ride to Kansas City Charlie still opined that Freedman wouldn't be so foolish as to stay so close to the border when he knew that he would he hunted down. Yet on second thoughts where else is a better place to go to hole than right under the noses of the hunters? If Freedman was in Kansas City, or wherever he was told he was, Charlie had decided, against his earlier decision, to take the risk of roping in Freedman alive. It would be a disappointment and a crying shame, he thought, after all the shooting he and Lars had had to do to get within one man of Lindford to kill that one man who could help to convict Lindford.

Alive, Freedman might still not sellout Lindford, dead, he definitely couldn't. Making him talk wasn't his problem, that task was Mr Jackson's. He had given himself the shit-detail of grabbing Freedman without killing him, or getting killed himself.

Charlie also got to wondering why he had called Lindford a Copperhead, a derogatory Union name, when they had both fought on the same side during the war. And looking on Lindford as an enemy of the Union. He was thinking like Liz Downes and her pa. Charlie smiled. Thinking like a President's man. Men who wanted to carry on the war, or to keep the distrust and hate going for their own personal gain, were a danger to the joining together of the two nations again and deserved the fate of traitors. Charlie's face hardened. By golly, he thought, he would grab Freedman, if he got the chance, as gently as a mother would lift her baby from out of its cot, so that he was in a fit state to talk. Then, round up

Lindford and end this business once and for all so that he could get back to the valley and spark up to Miss Liz Downes. The damn war was going on too long.

TWELVE

Freedman's escape plan had hit a snag, Lindford wasn't in Kansas City. On reaching town he had gone straight to Queenie Stewart's whorehouse knowing Lindford's regular days of cooling his blood by pleasuring his favourite girl. The Sporting House had been their regular meeting place. Mixing casually, passing the time of day with the rest of the establishment's clientele, before taking the girl of their choice upstairs to the private rooms. Keeping up the pretence of there only being a nodding acquaintance between them.

Freedman didn't ask Queenie Stewart where Lindford was when he noticed the big-breasted, tight-assed blonde, Lindford's girl, sitting on another client's knee. But, by keeping his ears open, he heard the blonde say that she would be free for the next two nights for anyone who fancied her. He left the whorehouse to do some urgent reassessing of his position.

Over a drink in the Buffalo's Head saloon Freedman thought fast but hard over his predicament. He had bought himself some time but in doing so he had directed the hunt on to him, and he knew the deadly efficiency of the Union Secret Service. He opined that his description would be known to them and by now Secret Service agents, Pinkertons could be heading this way from Washington by the trainload, out for his blood. Lindford, the man they were really hunting for, could sit on his big fat ass, smoking his expensive Havanas, till he was finally cornered. If he was killed Lindford would be in the clear. Taken alive, while it went against all his life's thinking, selling someone out to the Union, he would seriously have to think of himself. He wasn't about to be taken to the scaffold for a crime he didn't take part in.

The risk he was taking by waiting for Lindford to return to Kansas City was for purely financial reasons. Lindford owed him money. He would up the payment by putting it bluntly to Lindford that he owed him extra cash for sicking the Union Secret Service on to him on what had been his business. It was worth the wait, Freedman believed, because he was going to soak Lindford real hard, enough for him to start up some business when he had at last broken clear of his pursuers, or he could start talking to the Union agents.

Lars had been doing some heavy thinking and had come to a decision. The certainty that he wasn't going to sit in some damn rocking-chair and let the greenhorn Secret Service agent, Mr Bannack, do all the hard, dangerous work on his own. In this part of the Union a man's loyalty was difficult to judge and a carelessly asked question could get Mr Bannack dead. Lars had toyed with the idea of giving Charlie a letter signed by Secretary of State Seward saying that the bearer of the letter was a government agent and that all State authorities, law officers, army, were commanded to give him any assistance he needed, top priority. But the letter could rebound on Mr Bannack, Lars opined. A loose-mouthed town marshal, or army officer, could blab to his friends that a Secret Service agent was in town. If Mr Lindford got to hear that an agent was still snooping around his bailiwick Mr Bannack would certainly end up dead, Lindford would shoot dead half of Kansas to protect his image and status. And Miss Liz Downes would hate him for the rest of his life.

Lars got out of his bed and softly cursing and groaning dressed himself. He couldn't fix the harness of his hideaway gun on his arm or strap a gunbelt about him. He made do by stuffing both the derringer and the Colt in his pants top and dropping a handful of reloads for the two pistols into his shirt pocket. He would have to ask Mr Downes to saddle up his horse. Lars grimaced with pain, and m'be give him a hand to mount it. He caught up with Caleb and Liz working in the big barn and told them of his intentions. Caleb laid down the hayfork and close-eyed Lars.

'Mr Jackson,' he said, 'the older a man gets the more foolish he becomes. How long do you think you can stay up on a horse, one-winged and several busted ribs? If the horse gets a scare or stumbles, then you'll hit dirt real hard. And that won't do your wounds a heap of good.'

'I'm only riding as far as Lawrence, Mr Downes,' Lars said. 'And it ain't foolishness on my part to do so. It could be a matter of life or death.' Lars heard Liz's sudden intake of breath behind him. He turned to face her. 'Not only for Mr Bannack, Miss Downes,' he said. 'Though I reckon that's all you are worrying your pretty little head about.' Lars swung his gaze back on to Caleb. 'I'm talking about the life or death of the President.' Then he told them who he and Charlie were and the reason for them being in Kansas. 'We opine that Lindford is our man, we're convinced that he's behind all the raiding you farmers have been suffering. But, like him being linked with Booth, we can't prove it to satisfy a judge and jury. I'm hoping that Mr Bannack takes Freedman alive and m'be he can be persuaded, for a short prison sentence, to spill the beans regarding Lindford's illegal activities. I'd be happy to put Lindford behind bars for his land-grabbing deals. Mr Bannack is new at this game and could give himself away if I'm not around to keep an eye on him. Could land himself into a whole heap of trouble.'

'I told you that Lindford was no good, Pa!' Liz cried out. 'And you wanted to sell him our land!'

'I did that, Daughter,' Caleb said. 'I did that and I owe you an apology. The turncoat sure fooled us valley folk, him showin' the flag and all. But getting back to your situation, Mr Jackson, though you've got a strong reason for goin' that don't make your wounds any less painful. You're not fit to ride even as far as Lawrence, and that's a fact. And I reckon you know it.'

'I'll take him, Pa, in the buggy,' Liz said. She hard-eyed her pa as if daring him to stomp down on her suggestion.

Caleb couldn't deny his daughter her way. She had fought a damn sight harder than he had to hold on to the farm. He guessed, more important to her than saving a President's life, was that she was in love with Mr Bannack and, like the true plains breed she was, wanted to be beside her man in time of trouble. Proudly he said, 'You get what things you need, Liz, I'll see to getting the buggy ready and help Mr Jackson to pack.'

Charlie brushed off as much of the trail-dust on his clothes as he could then rubbed his scuffed, down-at-the-heel boots against the back of his pants before setting out to check out his only lead on Freedman in Kansas City, Queenie's whorehouse. He hoped that he didn't look too much like a saddletramp or he wouldn't get past Queenie's bouncer. If the lead petered out Charlie resolved himself to the ball-aching task of doing the rounds of all the saloons and hotels in his search for information about Freedman. Acting, according to Mr Lars, as a genuine agent, checking on every place that could yield a clue to Freedman's whereabouts. Then things came together for Charlie as he walked past the Buffalo's Head saloon, painfully and dramatically right.

The swing doors of the saloon pushed open and Freedman stepping out on to the boardwalk almost bumped into him. A startled Charlie clawed for his gun but Freedman, just as alarmed, was quicker in his reactions in finding himself face to face with his hunter. The knife that suddenly appeared in his right hand stabbed savagely at Charlie. Wildly Charlie flung himself sideways in a desperate attempt to escape the deadly blade and instead of getting the knife up to its hilt in his stomach, as Freedman had intended, it only gouged a deep, painful, but non-fatal, furrow above his left hip.

Sobbing, clutching at his side, Charlie dropped to his knees, folding in the middle like a burst feed sack. Through waves of sickening pain that brought curtains of blackness opening and closing in front of his eyes Charlie heard the boom of

his Colt and felt it kick in his hand
without realizing he had drawn it. He
also heard Freedman's dying shrieks as
the ball ripped into his groin and out
through the base of his spine before the
blackness overwhelmed him and he fell on
to his face.

'One of them, the knife-man, who got
himself killed was called Freedman, Captain,' Lindford heard the mayor tell the
army officer. 'A little fat fella, came in here
occasionally.' Lindford's hand holding the
glass of whisky froze halfway to his mouth
and suddenly he lost the burning urge to
take the blonde upstairs. He felt as though
his teeth were being pulled out one by one,
fully conscious, with blacksmith's pliers, as
the mayor droned on. 'You must have seen
him, he fancied Julie. The man he knifed
was a stranger to town. He's over at the
doc's, badly slashed, but OK. I heard
that when the marshal checked over the
stranger's gear to see if he could find
out his name he found a reb tunic in
his warbag.'

Lindford had heard enough dishearten-
ing news. He picked up his hat and all but
ran out of the whorehouse. Once outside
in the street he managed to get control
of his nerves, allowing him to stop and
lean back against a store front and light
up a cigar, albeit with hands that shook,
and took stock of his situation.

Reb tunic or not he was in no doubts
that the man Freedman had knifed was a
Union Secret Service agent. He couldn't
be the agent he had given instructions to
Freedman to kill because he would have
been known to the marshal as being the
barkeep in the Plains saloon. What the hell
had happened to him? The territory could
be swarming with Union agents. How on
earth had they got on to Freedman? Had
Freedman led them to him?

Lindford looked anxiously about him,
half-expecting to see Union agents closing
in on him. He was sweating as profusely as
though he was with the blonde, humping
her in her room. He straightened up from
the wall and tossed his cigar away. It was no
use standing here all night asking himself

questions he couldn't answer, action would have to be taken to prevent the hunt from getting any closer to him. This time he would do it himself.

Marshal Lucas looked up from his desk when Lindford came into his office. Lindford wasted no time to get to the reason of his visit.

'I hear that there's been a shooting in town, Marshal,' he said. 'And the man who did it is being treated by Doc Hall.'

'You heard right, Mr Lindford, though he ain't hurt bad,' the marshal replied. 'But he killed the fella he plugged.'

'You're not charging him with anything then?' Lindford said.

Marshal Lucas gave Lindford a look of surprise. 'What with? The man pulled a knife on him. He was only defending himself.'

'But who is he, Marshal,' Lindford's voice lowered into a serious, concerned pitch. 'I believe a reb tunic was found amongst his gear. It's my opinion that he is one of the marauders who have been raiding the border farms. What little

I know of Mr Freedman, the man he shot, was that he was a strong supporter of the Union cause. It could be that he got killed because he had stumbled on where the border scum have their hole-up and had to be silenced.' Lindford paused to let his forked-tongue words take root.

'Could be, Mr Lindford,' Marshal Lucas replied thoughtfully. 'There was no fightin' or arguin' between them. Just went for each other like a couple of mad dogs.'

'What is disturbing me, Marshal,' Lindford continued with his lies, 'is that the gang could ride into town to find out what has happened to him. Could turn Kansas City into another Lawrence.' He paused again, noticing with satisfaction the marshal's face-paling into a bloodless mask. Thinking, Lindford knew, of all the blood the marauders had spilt in Lawrence. 'Now I know you and your two deputies can't, and shouldn't, be expected to handle trouble that big,' Lindford said, sympathetically. 'But I'm willing to take him to my place; as you well know it is well guarded, keep him there till I can find out all about him. You can announce it publicly where he is being taken. That should get back to the rest of his gang and keep them from raising hell in your town, Marshal.' Lindford gave Marshal Lucas a drummer's oily smile. 'Of course it's your decision, Marshal, you are the law in Kansas City.'

Marshal Lucas could grab at a straw as well as the next man when he saw them floating past him. 'You take him, Mr Lindford. Technically he ain't under arrest so you just take him. You tell me though if you find out any law-breaking he may have done, to keep the record straight.'

Lindford favoured the marshal with a 'good dog' rewarding smile. 'A wise decision, Marshal, I'll arrange to have him picked up right away.' Under his breath he added that he had every intention of making the son-of-a-bitch talk. Talk till he told him who he was and how much he knew about Mr Thomas Magnus Lindford, and who else was backing him up.

THIRTEEN

Liz drew up the buggy outside the first livery barn she saw as she drove into Kansas City then she looked with concern at the drawn, pain-etched face of Lars. She could see by the growing crimson stain on his bandage that what she had feared had happened, the roughness of the trail had opened up his chest wound. It worried her. As had the news they picked up in Lawrence that Mr Bannack had shot one man and pistol-whipped another before leaving for Kansas City. One time, Liz thought frightenedly, Mr Bannack might not be able to walk away from trouble.

Lars was getting the same feelings; Mr Bannack had been stretching his luck to the limit. He had lost count of the dead and wounded they were leaving behind them. They were riding across the territory like Old Testament avenging angels bringing death to the Egyptians. Mr Lindford had proved a difficult and dangerous man to get close to. Lars groaned softly as Liz helped him out of the buggy. Liz decided that she could no longer hold in her concern for him.

'I know that you are worried that Mr Bannack could be heading into more trouble.' Liz gave a maidenly blush. 'No more than I am, Mr Jackson. But if you don't see a doctor and get your wound attended to it will be left to me to help Mr Bannack if things go bad for him. And I'm no gunfighter.'

Managing a ghost of a smile Lars said, 'You won't get any argument from me on that suggestion, Miss Downes. To tell the honest truth I wouldn't have made it to Lawrence on a horse. I'm beholden to you for getting me this far without me passing out on you. So it's only right I should see a doctor because looking out for Mr Bannack is my business.'

Liz sweet-smiled him. 'I'll see to it that the horse is fed and watered and wait for you here.'

'You're the second man I've had to patch up in the last couple of days,' Doctor Hall said after he had finished re-bandaging Lars' chest, 'A young fella brought in with a nasty knife slash across his thigh. Killed the man that cut him. There was talk of him being a Johnny Reb, a Missourian raider. Mr Lindford took him from the very chair you're sitting on; took him back to his ranch as precaution against the brush boys crossing over the border to effect his rescue.'

Lars got to his feet, face an ice-cold mask of suppressed anger, cursing inwardly for allowing Mr Bannack to trail Freedman on his own. His luck was bound to have run out. He should have wired Washington for more agents. He should have.... Lars stopped thinking about what he ought to have done and concentrated on things that had to be done, now. He thanked Doc Hall for treating him, giving him double the fee he had asked for. 'That will pay for the work you did on the reb kid.'

Doc Hall raised a quizzical eyebrow. 'He

did pay me, not the full amount, but it was all he had. Was he a special friend of yours?'

Lars' smile didn't soften his face any. 'Right now I'm not so sure.' And left Doc Hall still no wiser for his asking.

Liz had finished feeding the horse and was busy hitching it up to the buggy when Lars returned to the barn. She looked up and smiled at him. 'Is your....' her voice and smile faded away on seeing the expression on his face. 'It's Mr Bannack, he's been hurt!'

Lars put his good arm round Liz's shoulders as a comforting gesture. 'He's been hurt, but not seriously,' he said. 'Though Lindford's holding him at his ranch so we'll have to act fast.' Lars favoured her with a stern-eyed look. 'I hope that you are not going to fall apart on me, Miss Downes. Mr Bannack will have use for the buggy when we get him out.'

Liz bit at her lower lip, holding back from showing her fears. 'I'm OK, Mr Jackson, honestly.'

'Good,' replied Lars. 'Our next step is to get ourselves some help.'

The letter with its official signature shown to the sentry on duty at the army post's HQ, plus his fierce, stomping-man's glare got Lars into the office of Colonel Lawson, the post's commander, in double-quick time. The colonel looked up from his papers to give Lars a baleful glance, taking in, with arched eyebrows, the arm in a sling and the bulkiness of bandages about his uninvited visitor's belly. 'I'm a busy man,' he barked brusquely. 'So make what you've come to see me about quick.'

Lars handed him his warrant. 'Read that, Colonel, then I'll tell you why I'm here.' He gave the Colonel a stony-faced smile. 'It will take more than a few minutes.'

Colonel Lawson listened with goggle-eyed, open-mouthed interest as Lars told him of the hunting down of M, whom he knew, as certain as he could be, was Mr Thomas Magnus Lindford, and about Lindford's land-grabbing activities along the border and his taking of Charlie. 'I need an armed escort, Colonel,' Lars concluded. 'If I go on to Lindford's land on my own to free my agent and arrest Lindford, I'll be shot down on sight on Lindford's orders, as a raiding brush boy. And he'll be able to get away with it.'

Colonel Lawson didn't believe a word he had heard. Thomas M. Lindford a Copperhead? Why, the man was being hailed as the next State governor. The Secret Service agent's wounds must have addled his brains. Then he remembered the traitor, General Benedict Arnold, and how he had fooled everyone by going over to the British. The Secretary of State's letter was real enough and to go against a written command by a Secretary of State was asking for an instant court-martial for disobeying orders. Being a by-the-book soldier he could only agree to the agent's demands.

'I'll have a troop ready for moving out in ten minutes time, Mr Jackson,' he said.

'That will do fine, Colonel,' Lars replied. 'I'd be further obliged if you can have a horse saddled up for me.' Lars knew that Miss Downes wouldn't be too happy at being left behind but there could be lead flying about depending on where Lindford's men's loyalty lay. His and Mr Bannack's wounds came with their duty and pay. It wasn't Miss Downes' duty to put herself up as a target. Before leaving, Lars asked one of the troopers to fix the derringer spring-holster on to his left arm, giving Lars a sneaky, son-of-a-bitch grin as he did so. Then Lars told him to rip out the right sleeve of his coat so that he could get the coat on and buttoned up to hide the derringer. He was as ready, Lars thought, as a one-armed man could ever be, to meet what trouble lay ahead. He only hoped he could stay on the horse.

As the detail, led by the colonel himself, Lars riding at his side, came within sighting distance of Lindford's big house, five fast-riding horsemen closed in on them from their left. The colonel raised a hand to halt the small column and waited for the riders to come up to them.

'Some of Mr Lindford's crew, Mr Jackson,' he said. 'The big man in front is Burke, the straw boss.'

A widely grinning Burke pulled up alongside the colonel. 'You had us worried for a spell, Colonel. We spotted your dust and thought that you were a bunch of Missouri raiders payin' us a visit, being that we've got one of the bastards tied up in the hay barn. Mr Lindford warned us to keep an eye for any of his buddies, shoot them down like the mad dogs they are.'

'This man you've got tied up in your barn, is he OK?' Lars snapped at Burke, impatient to get Mr Bannack out of Lindford's clutches before he could do him more harm.

'Who the hell are you, mister?' said Burke, hard-eyeing him.

Colonel Lawson did the answering. 'He's Mr Jackson, a Union agent.' The colonel cleared his throat. 'He has something to tell you, Burke. You had better listen good.'

Lars didn't waste more time in lengthy explanations. 'Your boss is a Copperhead and I'm here to arrest him for being implicated in the plot to kill Lincoln. The so-called raider you're holding is one of my agents.'

Burke looked at Lars, ready to laugh off what he had heard, but could see no signs of humour in the gaunt, one-winged dude's Indian-face eyeballing him. He switched his gaze on to the colonel. 'Is it right what he says, Colonel?'

Po-faced, Colonel Lawson said, 'Mr Jackson's the man to put that question to, Burke. I'm in no position to confirm or deny it. I'm only here to see that he gets through to the big house unharmed.' And that's all he was damn well going to do, he thought. Lindford would raise one hell of stink when he was accused, right back to Washington. When the shit started to fly he didn't want any of it to land on him and ruin his career.

Burke did some heavy thinking, looking at Lars as he did so, before saying, 'I fought for the Union during the war, I ain't about to fight agin it now. You do what you've got to do, mister, though I think you're wrong on your readin' of Mr

Lindford. Two of my boys will go with you, show you where your man is. He's OK, but some of the crew roughed him a little. Came kinda natural to them havin' lost kin to the raiders.'

'That's understandable, Mr Burke,' Lars said, holding off showing his anger. 'I would be obliged if you would send a man back along the trail apiece. He'll find a girl, a Miss Downes, waiting there with a buggy. He's to tell her to come up to the ranch.'

Slowly, painfully, Charlie regained consciousness and found himself still bound hand and foot lying in the corner of the barn he had been thrown in. He recollected a big, fleshy-faced dude accompanied by four men coming into the surgery and, despite the doc's protests, being dragged out, hogtied, and slung over the back of a horse. The dude, he reckoned, must be Lindford. The rough treatment, the kicks in the ribs, the punches in the face, from Lindford's crew were, Charlie thought, only a foretaste of what was to come before Lindford had him killed. The hunter had become the prey. Yet, for all the pain, and his fears, Charlie hadn't regretted signing up as a President's man. He felt the pride of a man who, against all odds, has won a small battle, the unmasking of M. He could have got himself killed on his first bank raid and would never have had the pleasure of meeting up with Miss Liz Downes. A man had to be thankful in these troubled times for what small gifts came his way without moping on how things ought to be.

The barn door was suddenly flung open and Charlie braced himself for more pain coming his way. To his surprise his bonds were cut and he was helped gently on to his feet and led outside. The sunlight blinded his blurred, swollen-eyed vision and Charlie only saw Lars as a tall, shadowy outline. He tried to voice his relief and thanks but his cut and bruised lips couldn't form the words.

Bitter anger-lines cut deep into the corner of Lars' mouth. 'You're OK now, Charlie. You boys take him where he can get cleaned up. In a few minutes from now a buggy will come fireballing in and the girl driving it has a soft spot for him. She's a high-spirited girl and if she sees her boyfriend in that state she's liable to set fire to the big house, that's after she's plugged you two.'

Charlie, Charlie thought. The first time the iron-faced son-of-a-bitch had called him that. He must have been real worried about me. He tried to grin when he heard that Miss Downes was here but couldn't make it, but the pleasure of meeting her again eased some of the pain he was feeling.

Lindford heard a slight noise outside on the porch and swung round in his chair and saw a tall, haggard-faced man standing in the porch doorway. He didn't have to rack his brains any more thinking of where the Secret Service agent posing as a barkeep was. He was standing like Nemesis on his carpet. He noticed that his unexpected visitor had his gun hand in a sling so there was no need to reach for the pistol lying within reach on his desk top. He would hear what the bastard had to say, see if he had any evidence against him. If it was damaging he would gun him down. Here, on his ranch, he was judge, jury and executioner.

'I reckon you know who I am and why I'm here, Mr Lindford,' Lars said.

Lindford nodded, smiling mockingly. 'But you can't tie me in with the killing of President Lincoln.'

'Now what makes you think I was about to accuse you of that, Mr Lindford?' Lars said. 'I'm here to arrest you for hiring Missouri scum to drive Kansas farmers off their land so you can buy it up cheap, not for being a Copperhead. It won't get you hung but it will put you away for a long spell and that will satisfy me.'

Lindford's smile this time developed into a real belly laugh. 'On what grounds, mister, you've no proof? The same as you've no proof that I was a Copperhead.'

Lars gave him a devil's fearsome smile back. 'Not true, Mr Lindford. I'll admit that the man who could finger you, Freedman, is dead. But he was a careful man, looked out for himself. He kept a book of all the times he visited Mason, who, incidentally, is also dead, along with his boys, the money paid over, the farms they had to raid etc. Your fancy city lawyers won't be able to dig you out of that hole.'

Lindford rocked back in his chair, stunned as though he had been dealt a heavy blow in the stomach. His face twisted into savage lines of hate as he saw his whole world, his years of wheeling and dealing to get to the top, blown away like some Kansas sodbuster's barn in the path of a twister. Wildly he grabbed for his pistol to pump the whole six loads into the architect of his downfall.

Lars saw that his lies had worked, provoked Lindford into making it a showdown. He flicked his arm and the snub-nosed derringer came into view. Lindford's face showed a split-second of horrified surprise before the twin barrels flamed and roared and the two shells caved in his chest, knocking him and his chair over backwards.

Lars walked round the desk and looked

down at him, and the spreading bloodstain on the fancy, frilled-edged, white shirt. Lars could see Lindford's eyes still twitching as the last of his life drained out of him. Face like chiselled stone he said, 'I don't know whether or not you can hear me, Mr Lindford, but the gun that's put you on the fast train to hell is the same one that killed a great American. I reckon a man with a literary turn of mind would call that poetic justice.' He waited a moment or two longer till Lindford's eyes had stopped their fluttering then turned and walked out of the room, another assignment satisfactorily completed. He would have liked to have seen Lindford hanged but life was full of disappointments. Lindford had known that, the hard way. He notified Burke that he no longer had a boss then, on being told that Charlie was in the kitchen, went to seek him out.

Liz was bathing Charlie's face when Lars came into the kitchen and she paused long enough in her cleaning of Charlie's cuts and bruises to favour Lars with an angry look for allowing Charlie to be placed in so much danger. Which quickly softened when she saw the shape he was in.

'You look all in as well, Mr Jackson,' she said. 'Sit you down and I'll see to your wound dressing after I've finished tending to Charlie.'

'You needn't put yourself out, Miss Downes,' replied Lars. 'I've wires to send, paperwork to see to. If I was to sit down in that chair I'll be sitting there for the next two days.'

'I take it that Lindford is dead, Mr Jackson; I heard the shootin',' Charlie mouthed painfully. 'I thought that him being a brainy man he would have figured out that we had no solid proof on him being a Copperhead, or a dirty land-grabber. Dared you to take him to court to prove your case.'

'The way I saw it, Mr Bannack,' Lars said, 'I knew we couldn't get him for being linked with Booth so I told him I knew of his land-grabbing business deals with Mason.' Lars thin-smiled. 'I sort of hinted that Mr Freedman had left written proof of what Mason was doing for him.

That pushed him into a tight corner and he decided to make a fight of it with no lawyers present to confuse the issue. It could have been me lying back there in that room but justice, or whatever, came out on the side of the righteous for once.'

'I sure wouldn't like to play poker with you, Mr Jackson,' Charlie said. 'Not with that ace you're holdin' up your sleeve.'

Lars looked at Liz. 'I don't know if Mr Bannack has told you about the deal I made with him in Washington, Miss Downes. If he hasn't it doesn't matter, he has fully honoured it.' He smiled. 'So he's all yours now if you want him. Unless he wants to remain a President's man.'

'No offence, Mr Jackson, but no thanks,' Charlie said. 'I want to grow old gradually, not overnight.' He gave Liz a gap-toothed grin and took hold of her hand. 'I'm goin' back to being a sodbuster, here in Kansas.'

'I can't fault you for taking that decision, Mr Bannack,' Lars said. 'It's a much more peaceful life than the one you had in mind

218

when you crossed the Potomac. I'm finding the pace too hard to keep up with, that's for sure. It has been a pleasure to have you work with me. I couldn't have nailed Lindford otherwise. More than likely got myself killed.' Lars leaned down and kissed a surprised Liz on the cheek. 'I won't get to kiss the bride when the day comes, Mr Bannack,' he growled good-naturedly. 'So it's only right and proper I do it now.' Then wishing them both the best of luck he left them to moon over each other and plan their future lives together to ride back to Kansas City and send the express wire that would set Secretary Seward's mind at rest. Then, thought Lars, as red-hot arrows started digging into his chest again, hindering his breathing, he would lie up for a few days, in a bed. As he admitted to Mr Bannack and his intended, this assignment had aged him, too old to be having lumps shot out of him. That comforting thought, and his personal pride in not wanting to appear as a weak-backed eastern dude to his hard-riding escort, Lars hoped, would keep him upright in the saddle till he reached Kansas City.